RENDEZVOUS WITH DEATH

GIL HOGG

gilhogg.co.uk

Matador
9 Priory Business Park,
Wistow Road, Kibworth Beauchamp,
Leicestershire. LE8 0RX
Tel: 0116 279 2299
Email: books@troubador.co.uk
Web: www.troubador.co.uk/matador
Twitter: @matadorbooks

ISBN 978 1785892 769

British Library Cataloguing in Publication Data.
A catalogue record for this book is available from the British Library.

Printed and bound in the UK by TJ International, Padstow, Cornwall
Typeset in 12pt Bembo by Troubador Publishing Ltd, Leicester, UK

Matador is an imprint of Troubador Publishing Ltd

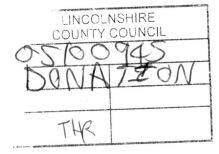

1

I had always had concerns about coming to Islamabad but it had turned out to be a mistake – literally, a hell of a mistake. Not only for me, but for Robert and Emma, too. Robert had persuaded me; he had melted my concerns and turned my reasoning into heresy. Think of it: leaving a legal practice in England to pursue a 'career' in one of the most troubled places on the planet – a cauldron of mutual hates and extremism.

I had now been in Islamabad for a few months as Robert Laidlaw's assistant. One afternoon, I entered his office in the High Commission building. He was absent. I dropped into a chair in front of the desk to wait, assuming he'd return in a minute or two. My eyes narrowed at the light from the garden. The faint dead-dog smell, the humidity, the cramped feeling of an inhospitable oasis made this a stark contrast to London – but it had its attractions. I had quickly acquired a taste for the ease of life and the laid-back pace of officialdom. I stretched languidly. I suppose it was because I was actually beginning to like what was negative and dangerous.

The room was redolent of Robert, infused with his grandiose personality. A confidential file of negotiations with the Kabul Government was open on the desk, and a fountain pen, uncapped, was lying on top (Robert disdained computers). The pen was valuable – platinum – and inscribed by well-wishers in Robert's former political constituency in the Midlands. One of the desk drawers was open. Inside was a box of small Dutch cigars with elaborate bands like signet rings, which Robert liked to smoke when he was working. The high-backed leather chair was swivelled to one side, as though he had just slipped out of it for a moment. A draught from the ceiling fan created the expectation of a presence. The room, shadowed by mahogany panelling, had a view of purple bougainvillea in the garden.

My own image was faintly reflected by the window pane and, with nothing else to do, I stared at it. The face was disappointingly undistinguished and commonplace – smooth, pale, straight-nosed, with small, active eyes under a pile of barley-coloured hair. It was a face that disguised a gold digger on the seam of great events, hoping for profit. I'd never admit that to anybody but myself. I felt insubstantial, a drifter with a half-formed idea of where I was going. Of course, I projected myself to other people very differently. I was a reliable lawyer, an efficient administrator, a calm hand– and this pseudo-Nicholas Dyson was well received. Or was I projecting the real Nicholas Dyson? The thought that I was aimless might really be no more than a well-suppressed and insubstantial fear.

I met the requirements of the Islamabad diplomatic establishment in my newly tailored, lightweight, dark blue suit, but contrived a suggestion of casualness in the loose way I wore my silk floral tie and soft-collared white shirt. I didn't think of myself as a Foreign Office or diplomatic type, but as an observer– a visitor for the time being.

I let my attention stray to Robert's collection of early Karachi etchings on the walls. The docks, factories and ships of the noble East India Company; colonialism captured as an attractive relic in half a dozen miniature windows. Silver-framed photographs on the bookcases showed important moments in Robert's political career: election victories; as a junior minister with the entire cabinet (Robert at the back, looking rather unimportant); with the Queen at his investiture as a knight. My eye glanced over the presentation items: the gold carriage clock, the Japanese sword, the engraved jade jar full of pencils; the lacquered cigar box; the crystal decanters (suitably full of Scotch and sherry)– all prizes that he had accumulated in his short career.

Robert Laidlaw was an important man by all the usual tests and I had a lot to gain from our association. He was possibly going to be the next ambassador to the United States and if not, the British nominee for a major appointment at the United Nations or in Europe– even a return to British politics wasn't ruled out. In any event, I calculated that I could surf on the crest of Robert's success. That's the sort of person I am when I wake from my sleep at 3am in the morning. It wasn't to be my success, but Robert's– and me with my hand in his pocket.

A century and a half ago, Robert might have made an excellent governor and commander-in-chief of a colony, carrying out his duties with a triumphant flourish. He was a plunderer by nature, with never a twinge of guilty self-effacement. And he would have looked so well in his whites, with the plumed cockade hat and that rubicund complexion. The glorious nonsense of empire would have been like wine to him. However, as that particular road wasn't open in this millenium, he had been promised as much by the Prime Minister. Well, not promised, but the Prime Minister had intimated the kind of opportunities that could lie ahead.

As special envoy to the Middle East and the Prime

Minister's personal trouble-shooter, Robert Laidlaw had influence. In realpolitik terms that made me, Nicholas Dyson, his personal assistant, much more considerable than I was as a junior barrister doing criminal work on the London and Southern circuit. The worthiness of my profession hadn't got through to me. Acting for sleazy clients, fencing with crooked solicitors and arguing revolting cases had strained my patience. I regarded myself as an accomplished liar, but the effrontery of the defendants' lies in the criminal courts was beyond sane belief. There were times when I wondered how I could stand before a judge and advance their absurd defences. And to be truthful, I wasn't doing very well. I could have done better if I had tried harder. Reflecting on it now, though, it hadn't been a bad life.

I became restive after waiting for a few minutes for Robert. I wanted to brief him on a meeting with officials of the World Bank, but he might go there directly. It was like him to change his plans without notice and to leave confidential papers in full view. He had none of the bureaucratic sense of order that I had assumed in my post. I closed the file on the desk, locked it in a cabinet and slipped the fountain pen into a drawer. I went into the adjoining office and asked Rashida Masood, Robert's secretary, to mention that I'd called in for the briefing.

Back in my room, a corridor away, I busied himself with a pile of Foreign Office memoranda and emails. After about an hour, Rashida appeared in the doorway.

"Nick, I've had a call from a World Bank secretary, wanting to know if there's been some mistake about the meeting with Sir Robert."

"Not as far as I know."

"That's what I told her. He hasn't arrived at the conference room."

"Call her back. Say that perhaps there is some misunderstanding. Offer to look into it."

"But –"

"Don't let's put Robert in the wrong."

Robert had an irreverent streak; missing an important meeting with officials at the Bank wouldn't have bothered him. I sent Rashida away, dismissed the matter from my thoughts and settled in my chair to continue the assault on my emails.

I then started to prepare Robert's brief for a meeting with the Afghan government representatives, which was to be held in a fortnight in Kabul. These meetings generated a lot of talk with London and with commercial interests. There were differences of opinion. Money was involved, so passions were generated. Consequently, there were reams of letters, faxes, emails and continual phone calls. I delighted in this turmoil. Since Robert paid little attention to detail, I took it upon myself to speak for him, which he entirely accepted.

After an hour and a half of reading and drafting, my eyes were sore from the computer screen. I felt thirsty and was thinking of ordering a cup of coffee from Kahar, the man who looked after such matters on the floor, when Bradshaw, the Foreign Office's appointee to head Robert's secretariat, rang.

"Sorry to disturb your siesta, Nick. A game over at the club?"

It was half past four. I found the little, rotund diplomat's company congenial. I appreciated that Bradshaw never made an issue about being pushed aside by me. He was officially Robert's number two, but in practice I was. Bradshaw may have been quietly plotting my downfall, but he was still amusing company. I agreed to his suggestion and closed the computer file.

"Hasn't taken you long to become infected by our pernicious habits, Nick," Bradshaw said, pleased yet critical.

I was well up on the preparations for Kabul and the idea of relaxing on the terrace of the Pakistan Club with a chilled beer and a game of backgammon was attractive. I put pleasure first, if possible, and wasn't troubled to hide it.

Bradshaw was gay, cattily charming even when delivering tepid insults, something of a sadist in attitude and tetchy without a mate. His shrewd, bald head, with eyes submerged in slits, sat atop a voluminous white shirt with jewelled cufflinks (our jackets were off).

I spent the rest of the afternoon with him, at a table with shade and a view of the avenue of plane trees where the crows cawed. Complimentary french fries were served with curry sauce, while Bradshaw beat me repeatedly at backgammon and several hands of poker. It puffed Bradshaw up to win and I didn't care. I wasn't very competitive, unless I felt it was important to show that I was.

When we finished our last game, Bradshaw said, "How's the mission, Nick?"

The fact that I didn't have any emotional commitment to the causes we espoused was something I never revealed, although Bradshaw may have guessed. To me, my work was like a case, a brief, to be argued and pushed as far as I could take it— provided I was paid for it. Always inherently interesting, it was a kind of game. To Bradshaw, however, it was the nervy grind of following the book and hoping for promotion.

"Since you ask, how would you define Robert's mission?" I replied.

"Very simply and I hope it's engraved upon your heart. Robert's task is to smooth the relationship with the Pakistanis, Iraqis and Afghans, to act as a midwife in the birth of democracies, to watch our American friends, and to obtain lucrative contracts for British industry."

"Those are in reverse order of importance, I suppose."

"Unquestionably. You're going to fit in here very well, Nick."

The air was soporifically heavy. I drew a deep breath and smelt the alien smell I'd first noticed when I'd stepped off the Boeing 747 from London at Islamabad Airport eight months ago. After I'd been here a while, I noticed the smell was everywhere— sometimes partially smothered by other odours, like that of the floor polish on the gleaming tiles of my office.

"What is that stink?" I asked.

"Oh, that. It's the Pindi smell," Bradshaw smiled. "Just as other cities have their own peculiar tang so does this one— mostly in spring and summer. A potpourri of damp foliage, filthy drains, exhaust fumes and cooking spices. Quite original, wouldn't you say? The inhabitants here call it the Pindi smell. They blame the sister city without hesitation. Nothing's quite like the sweat of Rawalpindi."

I turned my glance from the table to my fellow idlers, perhaps businessmen doing deals, and beyond them, over the white stone balustrade of the club's terrace, to the city offices and gardens. I was pleasantly conscious of how close I was to the throb of this diplomatic enclave without actually being involved. I shook my head. That was wrong. I was involved, however abstracted I felt. The involvement was like putrid water soaking my feet and likely to rise. Why were we here? What were we actually doing?

At six o'clock, my driver took me to my apartment on the higher ground above the city, near Kashif Gap. The driver, the car and the apartment all came with the job as

Robert's personal assistant. It was excessive and ridiculous, but I would have fought anyone who tried to take it away. The car climbed up the Kashif Road, passing the pale and spacious buildings of the diplomatic quarter, then the elegant apartments and gardens that had been chiselled out of the slope. As we ascended, I was freed from any view of the squalor that spread out around the twin cities. From this distance, Islamabad and Rawalpindi receded into a haze, pierced only by occasional tall buildings and minarets. I was carried up to a land of carefully reared trees, flower gardens of studied colours, and apartments with wide views of the skies and mountains above the haze. The shanties of Rawalpindi and the ragged kids with their hollow chests were a mere memory.

My apartment was on the fifth floor of a block, set on generous lawns shared with two other blocks, with a view to the south over bush-covered slopes. This area was virtually a British territory. We didn't own Pakistan any more, but we had reserved ourselves parking spaces. The apartments were high enough to escape the smog and be apart from the twin cities. Mine had bedrooms and terraces that I would never use; it was quite a splendid spread for a bachelor. Such luxuries were seductive. I groaned whenever I remembered the poky rooms I used to have in Fulham, London, and the monthly struggle to prioritise the champagne bill or the rent.

I showered and changed into shorts and a T-shirt. The slight draught was sultry, but not unpleasant. I padded through the rooms on their woodblock tiles in bare feet. Ashraf kept the place scrupulously clean. I could hear him clattering dishes in the kitchen, preparing dinner. Here was the enjoyable part of being an expat.

I had just fixed myself a Scotch and ice when Emma Laidlaw, Robert's wife, rang. It was 7pm.

"Bob and I have a cocktail party tonight, Nick, at the German Embassy and he said he'd be home around six. His office isn't answering. Where is he?" Emma asked, characteristically cool and demanding.

"I haven't seen him since this morning, Emma, but I'm here. Why don't we party together?"

"Damn you, Nick. You're never serious!" She swore and slammed the phone down.

We knew each other well enough for that. I tried to put Emma out of my thoughts as I took a seat alone at the head of my dining table. The table, a fine piece of local craftsmanship, that was polished and inlaid with Islamic designs, deserved guests. Ashraf began to serve dinner. A slice of cold melon to start, followed by steak with fried noodles. The noodles, slightly seasoned with oregano and garlic, were delicious.

I had tried to explain to Ashraf, who was a wise-looking man of about forty, with a face as round and brown as a pancake, that if steak was grilled for more than a few minutes it was like leather. Ashraf had smiled (my interpretation of the lines on his cheeks) and nodded as if he had understood, before continuing to produce exactly the same steak– which I presume he had been preparing for various masters and mistresses for years.

As I chewed the tough meat, Emma's image returned. Dark, shoulder-length hair with shining natural waves; tanned skin; provocative and quite large brown eyes; and a revealing, expensive frock, probably in cream or white. Emma had a small body, but she had shape– in her calves and small ankles and pert breasts. And she was soft, as though her bones were made of rubber. I could see her twirling impatiently in front of her bedroom mirror while she waited for her husband. Her expression unlined, but resolving occasionally into a bitchy glare.

At midnight, Emma Laidlaw called again. It woke me. The bed lamp was on. I had fallen asleep, reading.

"Where the devil is he?" she asked savagely, without any polite preliminaries.

"I have no idea, Emma. I'm not his keeper." I wasn't irritated. Emma in a temper was better than no Emma at all.

"Oh, Nick, he's a lousy bastard! Leaving me high and dry like that, in front of Lady Leighton, the crabby old cow. I was late. 'Where's your charming husband, my dear?' she wanted to know.'I haven't a bloody clue!' I said."

Emma's voice, even in a rage, made me tingle. "You should have asked me to take you."

"I'm serious, Nick."

"OK, I'll try to raise Petrie," I said in a businesslike tone.

I was reluctant because I was well aware of Robert's penchant for having a good time and letting everyone else and everything else go to hell. You always had to wait for Robert, but he would always appear at last, grinning – and late.

"Huh!" Emma scoffed. "They're probably out whoring together."

"Probably. You ought to find some consolation."

"I may take you up on that!" she said and rang off abruptly.

I lay awake and wondered if Robert had suddenly decided to go on a jaunt. It was quite possible. Emma wasn't really worried– anger and frustration would be nearer the mark. Islamabad was a place that interesting people often passed through. There were always opportunities for a surprise dinner engagement, or a few drinks with a new arrival.

After some time, I decided it would be worthwhile to call Petrie as I'd promised. The Special Branch officer was

Robert's bodyguard– security adviser was the official title. I had Petrie's home number. A little after midnight was an unsocial time, but he was a cop. A woman answered the telephone immediately. She was English, from Lancashire probably, and wide awake. I reminded her who I was. She remembered meeting me at a departmental drinks party.

"I'm afraid Sir Robert hasn't shown up this evening. I thought Jim might know where he is," I said calmly, only a little exasperated at the bother.

"Jim's not home, Mr Dyson. I haven't heard from him. He's usually pretty good at keeping in touch. I know he had to go to a party with Sir Robert tonight. I thought it was cocktails. I had his dinner ready for 10.30pm."

"Oh, well, just a little delay along the line," I said breezily. "They'll turn up."

I didn't want to worry her. At this time, there was literally nobody I could chase. I could call Hall, the top Special Branch man, but that seemed excessive. I decided against ringing Emma to report. She'd only explode. It was possible that Robert had suffered some kind of accident or injury, but he wasn't alone. If I called the police and they found out that Robert was a big British chief, there would be a fuss, which would transmit itself to all sorts of quarters. Nobody at the High Commission could do anything useful at this time. Although it wasn't yet 1am, the night had hardly begun for some people in Islamabad and Rawalpindi. It was most likely that Robert was in one of the dozens of clubs, absolutely undiscoverable. In fact, it might be embarrassing to find him.

I dozed off, thinking how inconsiderate Robert could be and how Petrie needed a kick in the backside for not reporting to Emma Laidlaw.

2

I was awakened at 7am by the humming of the air-conditioning unit. I was vaguely uneasy and then remembered what a nuisance Robert could be.

I showered, dressed in another new suit (this time, dark grey) and took my time at breakfast. If Ashraf was a failure with steak, he was a star with eggs. I ordered them scrambled, and they were served firm but creamy in texture. The brown toast came with a tasty jam I couldn't identify. At first, Ashraf said it was strawberry, but on a later day he said it was gooseberry.

While I drank my coffee, I watched the BBC World Service news and then switched to the *Islamabad Daily Mail's* online news. A suicide bomber in Karachi; US drones killing on the Afghanistan border with Pakistan; and a further reduction in the US training contingent in Afghanistan. The British withdrawal from Helmand seemed a long time ago. There was a short but flattering article on Robert that also mentioned a certain Nicholas Dyson. We were becoming a pair already. While I'm good at complicated negotiations, because I can remember the details of all the thirty or so files we are running, Robert is a broad brush man– testy with detail, but with an instinct for the real point. In a year or so from now, a lot more people will have heard of Robert and me. The article said that Robert was making a helpful contribution to the stability of governments in Iraq and Afghanistan, and that his efforts were welcome. The usual warm soapy water. The paper naturally made no mention of the contracts for arms and construction equipment that we had facilitated, or the aid we had directed into the hands of government ministers in Kabul.

After 8am I rang Robert at his apartment, intending to point out delicately the difficulty he had caused with the World Bank officials. I'm not afraid of Robert, but I'm candidly respectful. I also wanted to let him know that I wouldn't be in the office. I had arranged a meeting with a group of engineering contractors followed by lunch with them and the flirtatious Pakistani woman who handled their public relations. It was a day that promised useful information, possible profit for Britain, a sparkle of wine and a frisson of sex.

While I was waiting for the phone connection, I could see the drape of my suit in the hall mirror– not bad. I moved my shoulders, approving the work of the Pakistani tailor. The difference between a tailored suit, even these cheap-jack local ones of mine, and an off-the-peg job was considerable. I couldn't have afforded tailored suits in London– what a dog I must have looked in my baggy, slump-shouldered, machine-made pinstripes.

"Emma? Nick. Robert, please?"

"Not a bloody sign of him!" she said in a low voice through clenched teeth.

I was surprised. What had seemed like Robert just messing about could now be something else. "Are you worried?"

I could hear Emma's steady breathing. "I'm annoyed. Swanning off like this. Are you worried? For Christ's sake, you're working with him!"

"Not really."

It was true. What was one night in Islamapindi? Robert

and I had gambled all night and until noon the following day more than once since my arrival. And Robert had his minder.

"Nothing bothers you, does it, Nick? If Robert comes reeling in here at ten this morning with a hangover, I tell you, I'll shoot the bugger. I've got a gun and I've had enough!"

I laughed. "Make sure you hit him in the balls!"

A car horn blasted from below and I said goodbye to Emma, or rather, she slammed the phone down. I walked through the open doors onto the terrace and looked over the rail. I smelt jasmine – unaccountably, being at such a height above the gardens. My car and driver were below. I hurried to the lift. It was a hot clear day and it was going to be interesting.

The car carried me down the hills, through and under a coverlet of smog on the Kashif Road, skirted the city and entered the wide, green diplomatic quarter. The driver pulled in through concrete security barriers to the entrance portico of the High Commission building. I got out, passed the security guards– who recognised me now– and climbed the stairs to Robert's office.

The room appeared to be almost the same as I had left it the previous afternoon. There was a slight smell of disinfectant. The meticulous cleaners had been at work, polishing and dusting. I went round to Robert's side of the desk and sat swinging a leg in the regal chair for a moment while I thought what to do. Idly, I pulled open the drawer in front of me. It was stuffed with stubs of pencils, erasers, clips and tape. On top was an envelope. I slid my finger in the opening of the envelope and saw a slip of paper. I withdrew the paper covertly and held it below the level of the desk in case anybody came in. It contained no address and was handwritten by Robert on quality notepaper.

Dearest C, I'm looking forward to meeting you for lunch on Wednesday. It seems a very long time…

That was all. I could imagine Robert in some romantic passion, straining for words and giving up in exasperation. He wasn't a writer. He lacked the imagination, although he was an eloquent speaker.

Wednesday was yesterday. While I considered, I became aware of the carriage clock ticking amid Robert's artifacts. The office drifted eerily on, though it was deserted. The thought that he could vanish in the tumult of this country and never be seen again came to me. This was just the sort of place where you could disappear. The throng churned in the streets, drawing passers-by into a vast squirming press. Robert wasn't the disappearing kind, though. He would protest too loudly.

I replaced the unfinished note and picked up a silver-framed photograph that was positioned prominently on the desk. It was a snap of Robert and Emma at Henley Royal Regatta, wearing straw boaters with ribbons on their lapels. The couple looked elegant and happy. Perhaps that was an illusion, although they were certainly elegant. Robert had other women, but he also liked to advertise that he had a striking wife. She was one of his political accessories.

Robert himself was startling, too, with his satyr's grin, slightly squashed nose, tousled blond hair and blue eyes like laser beams. He presented himself as the archetypal middle-class English politician: public school, Cambridge, the City. Underneath, well concealed, was the rough, unscrupulous sensualist with a metallic skin that I also knew. However, he was very likeable and, for me, mesmeric.

Packing up life in England and coming to Pakistan

had been easy for Robert because he had had experience of colonial life. His father had served in various colonial and Commonwealth posts, and had ended his career as Solicitor General in Hong Kong when it was a colony. A small photograph of him in wig and gown was on a side table. Robert had spent a lot of time flying backwards and forwards to school and university in England. In many ways he was an inspired choice for the task of special envoy. He understood the aspirations of the Anglo Pakistani elite who controlled Pakistan's economy, having been marinated in those aspirations over many years.

"Hello. You've taken over now, have you, Nick?"

I replaced the picture. Rashida Masood stood in the doorway in her high heels and tight skirt, a hand on one hip. She was a coquettish woman of about my age. She called me by my first name when we were alone. Otherwise protocol dictated that I was entitled to 'Mr'.

"Just waiting for Robert," I said.

I stared at her. Her attractions disrupted my thoughts: the cleft of her bosom, the thick but nobly carved features of her dark face, the shining surfaces of her succulent lips. I felt that we had secretly, and without a word being said on either side, marked each other for a dalliance on a future day– if it proved possible. It would be complicated, though. Rashida would no doubt be concerned at disturbing the relationship with her handsome, half-English, surveyor husband.

"Sir Robert never came back yesterday," she said in an untroubled tone.

"Did anybody call here for him at around lunchtime?"

"Why are you asking?" She had a mischievous look, as though I was being nosey.

"Because he never arrived home last night."

She shrugged, unconcerned. "Well, I don't know anything."

I was unconvinced; it was the secretary being discreet about her boss. "Who did he leave with, Rashida?" I asked crossly.

The pulse of her attraction switched off. She walked out. I sighed. I was beginning to learn that women from the sub-continent– even the Anglophiles– withdrew where a Western woman would, if necessary, stand her ground or flare up.

Frowning at my clumsiness, I walked a few doors along the corridor to the office of Jim Petrie, the Special Branch man. Perhaps he, at least, had surfaced. He had always seemed to me to be more like CID than Special Branch. You could spot him in a crowd at 20 yards: tall and muscular in a plain dark suit, a dark tie and white shirt; bristling short fair hair, a bony face and accusing eyes. At this time of day he was likely to be squatting at his desk studying the morning emails in his white shirtsleeves, his hands with bitten fingernails clasped on a notebook. Petrie was a reassuring presence.

A Pakistani clerk in his office greeted me. "Inspector Petrie hasn't been in this morning, Mr Dyson."

"When did you last see him, Ahmed?"

"I brought him sandwiches for lunch in his office at about noon yesterday."

"Did he stay and eat them?"

"No, sir. He left them. I cleared away last night."

So Petrie had gone with Robert to the luncheon engagement with C. I went back to my office and telephoned Petrie's partner. She was on the verge of tears. I tried to soothe her. "As soon as I hear anything, Dawn, I'll have somebody call you. I'm sure there's nothing to worry about."

I looked out of the window at the gardeners pruning

the hibiscus tree on the lawn, their faces as composed as if they were meditating. If I reported Robert missing to Hugh Leighton, the High Commissioner or to the head of Special Branch, there would be embarrassment, raised eyebrows and gossip when Robert returned. He would be annoyed. It was curious, though, that neither his wife nor secretary nor Petrie's partner nor I knew anything at all. If some kind of accident, or even abduction, had befallen them, the sooner the alarm was given the better.

I made my decision and called the head of Special Branch, Chief Superintendent Hall. I had met him regularly at the political briefings I attended with Robert. I had to insist that Hall was disturbed in a meeting to take the call.

"This might be very important, Leonard, or it might be nothing," I said. "Robert has been missing since yesterday around midday and your man, Petrie, too. Neither were at home last night. Their wives are worried. They may have gone on a binge, but it's also possible…"

I heard a long indrawn breath as the political cop assessed the problem. "I'll be right there," croaked Hall. His compressed response was full of every awkward and awful possibility.

I was still doubtful about having called Hall when he arrived, half an hour later. He stood on the threshold of my office, silent, with a demanding stare, as though Robert's failure to appear was my fault.

"We better keep this quiet until we're sure something's wrong," I said, cautiously.

"I'll decide that."

Hall, thin and slightly stooped, wearing a faded grey suit that hung loosely on his frame, twitched bleakly. He didn't need a lesson from a new boy. We walked to Robert's office and went in. Hall circled the desk warily without getting too close. His long, white fingers with big joints waved impotently in the air.

"When I came in yesterday, Leonard, there was a confidential file open on the desk and Robert's personal fountain pen. It looked as though he'd gone to the john."

"No sign of him since? No note or phone call?"

"Nothing. He stood up a meeting with the World Bank."

"Didn't that make you suspicious?"

"No. Robert sometimes does that with meetings. I didn't have any reason to see him for the rest of the day. Lady Laidlaw rang me in the evening."

"Why didn't you report to me then?"

"I wasn't worried and she wasn't worried. She was annoyed."

"Jesus, man," Hall said, tiredly, "this is a dangerous place. Surely, you thought of the possibilities. We're all at risk, but Laidlaw more than most."

"I rang Petrie's partner around 1pm. We both thought they'd been held up somewhere."

"Oh, come on, Dyson! If you were half awake, you would have called me at close of business yesterday."

Hall was looking for somebody to blame. "Hindsight. I didn't and I don't see it that way."

I understood that Hall was measuring the extent of aggravation he would have to suffer if Robert really had disappeared. It meant publicity, official enquiries, media comment– and it would be his personal responsibility to find Robert. If he had been seized by terrorists, the likely outcome was death, but Hall had no sympathy. He was just concerned with the trouble it would cause him.

"I'll put on a small team to check everything, but we should have got to work yesterday."

I swallowed the rebuke. "Robert will probably turn up like a wandering tomcat."

Hall responded with a weak smile, which was incapable of lifting the down-turned corners of his mouth. "I certainly hope so, for all our sakes."

"Who would do this, if it's an abduction?"

Hall looked at me, his thin face sunken and curiously pale despite a lifetime in the East. "If Laidlaw's been abducted, it's unlikely to be criminals looking for a ransom. This isn't Somalia. And why go for a government man when you can get a millionaire shipowner or a property magnate? No sense in that."

"So, politicals?"

He walked out without giving me the courtesy of an answer.

I went back to my office, worried. Hall could be right. Terrorist outrages were common here. The murder of Daniel Pearl had happened some time ago. Robert knew his appointment made him a prime target and he was inclined to take it rather lightly. His death would be a kick at the British for dabbling in Iraq and Afghanistan. And Robert would have made enemies. In time-honoured imperialist fashion, on behalf of his masters, he had plunged his hands deep into the meat barrel of the redevelopment contracts and financial aid that the wars had generated. There were many contenders, but not everybody could be favoured with lucrative contracts or an attractive aid package.

I couldn't help but be struck by how this could affect me. Robert only needed to survive and the two of us would be near the top of the tree of international government. It was an exciting prospect. Now, however, this non-appearance–

which seemed to be becoming a disappearance– was like a grain of sand in my usually buoyant mind.

I went into Rashida Masood's office. "I'm sorry if I upset you with my question about Robert. I'm worried, that's all."

"It's OK," she smiled, sitting up, pushing out her chest and reverting to her come-on signals.

"He left with a woman?"

She opened her eyes and then, with a coarsely salacious look, glanced down and carried on with her word processing. So Robert was with a woman. All this would come out. The next step was to tell Bradshaw. I went downstairs to Bradshaw's office, entered and sat down without waiting to be asked. He was always affable and there was nothing he liked better than to philosophise over a cup of coffee about anything in the cosmos except work – there, he was always flippant.

"What's the latest?" he asked, gladly pushing aside his papers and ringing the bell for Kahar. "You're rather unseasonably serious."

"Robert's missing."

"Gone walkabout, has he? What about his minder?" Bradshaw grinned.

"Petrie's missing, too."

"So? They like to party."

"This could be serious, Geoff."

I explained what I knew and Bradshaw's benignity did not change, though his eyes glinted in near-concealment behind horn-rimmed spectacles. He was keenly interested and, I thought, still ambitious beneath his frivolous exterior. He obviously felt that if anything happened to the envoy, he would be able to take a more prominent place in the talks. Judging from the hints mentioned during my earlier conversations with him, it would be a distinction he would welcome. Indeed, it might boost him to head a high commission or even a lesser ambassadorship. He had been first secretary in two posts before this and was being overtaken by younger men.

"An empty chair and a puff of cigar smoke in the air. What shall we do about it?" he asked, casually.

"Special Branch are on the job."

"That's a recipe for confusion."

"Is there anything else but Special Branch?"

"No, we can't call Ghafoor's Discreet Detective Agency. We're neutered. Nick, I wish you'd told me before you called Leonard," he said. His expression turned sour.

"Why?" I asked, still smarting from Leonard Hall's criticism.

"Because I'm Robert's number two and I report directly to London."

"Oh, shit! Hall was also whining about not being told early enough! And now you're telling me…"

"You do get the point, old lad, don't you?"

"Yeah. Lines of communication."

"It may be frightful codswallop, Nick, but that's the way we do it. As formal as a foxtrot."

"Leonard Hall thinks Robert could have been abducted by terrorists," I said, trying a different tack.

"No point in speculating," Bradshaw said, trying to show that he really wasn't that concerned.

I thought, however, that he was already contemplating the potential advantages of Robert's disappearance. We sipped the scalding hot (and vile) coffee, which I was becoming addicted to, in silence. I had found that Bradshaw had no serious opinions except regarding wine and manners. In that sense he was utterly discreet and predictable, like a butler or a head waiter. It was his refuge against the disappointments in his career.

"Perhaps an Al Qaeda or ISIS group is trying to torpedo our efforts," I persisted.

"Perhaps, perhaps. No shortage of people aggrieved with us. A few warlords, disappointed Afghan and Pakistani politicians and their families, and business interests outside the Anglo-US breadbasket – oh, yes."

"I suppose some people in London might like Robert to disappear." I thought back to how he had been parachuted into the job by the Prime Minister, which had no doubt sent tremors of disaffection through the FO hierarchy.

"I daresay," Bradshaw echoed, with a theatrical sigh.

"And there's a wedge of British opinion that has hardened against the campaigns in Iraq and Afghanistan." I watched Bradshaw's reactions.

Bradshaw lay back in his chair, coffee cup in hand. "The trouble is, democracy is a slightly suspect word around here. A flunky state, loaded with debt. The natives don't want to hear a Brit, or an American for that matter, chanting about it. What the natives rightly see, cloaked in red, white and blue, is secular nationalism. The late Mr Qutb has told them that that's poison and what they really need is an Islamic community– an ummah."

"That makes a monkey of Robert's mission."

"Not entirely, Nicholas. I told you what Robert's mission was and the ultimate purpose of it is to make sure that Britain is on the side of the angels."

"You mean the side with the most contracts for reinstatement?"

Bradshaw's round head wore a sarcastic, moon-like grin. "I'm afraid Sir Robert has stepped into a vortex of political forces– with great panache, of course!"

3

My career at the criminal bar in London hadn't gone well. The competition between barristers in my chambers had been fierce and I had had to admit to myself after a time that I didn't have the histrionic gifts that would give me prominence. I wasn't a play-actor or a bully. I didn't take to the pressured lifestyle either, travelling around to court hearings in the day and studying criminal briefs at night. It was like having my nose in a sewer, in which guns, knives and hypodermic needles were submerged. I was typecast by the specialty of my chambers; it was criminal work or nothing. The more lucrative civil cases went to those with better connections and qualifications in different chambers. The likelihood of moving upstream to civil chambers, without the assistance of friends or some intellectual distinction, was negligible. Therefore, accepting the job of personal assistant to an important diplomatic envoy was a sensible career move.

Robert had been chosen by the Prime Minister as envoy not because he was a distinguished diplomat or linguist, but because his promising career in the House of Commons had been spoiled by the loss of his seat. The loss was no fault of Robert's, nor was it a whim of the voters. A boundary change in a seat that was never safe had cost him his place. He had been a convincing young politician and it would take time to find him a safe seat at Westminster. In the meantime, there was an opportunity to make a name for himself as an envoy– and plenty of time for a man in his early thirties to return to Parliament.

Robert received his knighthood, as a thank-you for his political services and in recognition of the importance of his new role as special envoy. The Foreign Office had been against his appointment as they had a number of people who would have made a more suitable envoy. They were equally against any henchman Robert might want to accompany him. The Foreign Office could supply all the assistance any envoy would need in someone like Bradshaw, but Robert had insisted on me and the Prime Minister had agreed.

For purely personal reasons I should have resisted Robert's invitation, but I didn't and couldn't. I had always found him difficult to resist– and then there was Emma, who was a kind of magnet to me. Joining with Robert linked me closely, uncomfortably closely, with the past and a small voice in me said that this should be avoided. That same voice, however, was overcome by Robert's flattering insistence and the pragmatic opportunity of the job. I contained my trepidation. 'I want somebody I can trust close to me when I'm dealing with those two-faced FO types and near-the-knuckle businessmen, Nick,' he had said, with his beaten-up smile.

We were friends, but Robert, a few years older, was always boss. I was a courtier, one of the audience he tended to gather. I couldn't define the bond between us, but, for me, it was like an invisible wire that could pull taut suddenly and cut into me.

Many people have a period, often early in their lives, when they shine. Everything seems possible. It may be a sporting achievement or playing a musical instrument, or being a multi-talented head prefect at school. Later, the shine fades and disappears. The promise has gone. My period of shining came when I attended the Grange Preparatory School in Fordingbridge, Hampshire for four years and rose up the ranks to become head boy. In those days, and only in those days, when I was in my early teens, I seemed to have a lucky combination of skills that outmatched my peers. I was popular and influential among the boys, always cheerful, a passable cricketer, probably the best rugby player in the school and in the top half dozen at lessons.

Being head boy made me bigheaded and later, when I went on to public school at Poole Abbey in Dorset, although I had no inkling of it at the time, I was bound to be cut down. Poole Abbey was one of the best known public schools in the south of England, and still is. On my first day there, I had taken the train from Salisbury– where I lived during school vacations with my maiden aunt– with the confidence of a young prince. My credentials were, after all, impeccable.

My father was then a brigadier with NATO in Germany. I never saw much of him, as he was always travelling to remote places. I was an only child. My mother had died when I was three. While this might suggest a lonely and deprived upbringing, the reverse had been the case. My relationship with my aunt was kindly, though distant. I never missed my father, because I never knew what it would be like to have him as a constant presence. I felt it a relief to be beyond parental control when I saw the paternal yoke on my friends.

My destination that day had been the town of Sherborne– not too far along the line, but, to me, with my bags and cabin trunk, it was like crossing the Alps on the back of an elephant. I took a cab from the railway station to Poole Abbey's March House, which I had been destined to attend ever since my father had submitted my name when I was about five. The house stood in a quiet street in the town, a quarter of a mile from the main school buildings. It was a handsome, fawn-coloured sandstone structure, which had been erected in the middle of the nineteenth century. Behind a spiked iron rail at the front was a small, cobbled courtyard. At one side of the façade, an archway led to the rear – where, at one time, there would have been stables.

When I scrambled out of the cab and started to tug at my trunk, some boys came out of the archway, picked it up and carried it through to the cloakroom at the back of the house. I can recall the smell of the room to this day: soap and sweaty gym shoes. The cloakroom seemed very dark after the brightness of the sun. The housemaster, James Larsen, appeared, mumbled a greeting and disappeared. In my years at Poole Abbey, Larsen and the other masters were never much more than creatures baying at the edge of my consciousness. It was to be a fierce world of boys and some girls.

I waited in the half-dark of the cloakroom, not quite knowing what to do, but trying to look at ease. Everybody was attending to their own business, coming and going, carrying armfuls of books, suitcases and sports gear. I felt a sense of anti-climax. I had expected a rather more formal welcome. A boy suddenly picked up my tennis racket, which had been resting against the trunk, and announced he was going to try it out at the courts. I grabbed him by the collar and snatched it back.

"Do you want your teeth knocked down your throat?" I said, loudly.

The boys nearby were silenced for a moment.

"I don't expect he does," said a voice behind me, "but why don't you go ahead?"

27

The boys laughed. I turned to the speaker. He was an older boy, his nose slightly flattened from rugby or boxing, tall, with alive eyes and the kind of brown-gold hair (like mine) that is so common at schools like Poole Abbey it could almost be a matter of regulation. I made no move. The Grange had prepared me for aggressive confrontations.

"Order may have been maintained at your last school by knocking teeth down throats, but this is a civilised society, understand?" the speaker said.

This comment brought a loud guffaw from the more seasoned watchers. It was a remark that always welled up later when I thought of these years: a civilised society.

"I'm Laidlaw," the speaker said, grinning when he saw my bemused stare. He then moved away quickly, as though on important business.

When I looked down, I saw that my tennis racket had gone from where I had replaced it on the top of my trunk.

"It wasn't me!" the original taker sneered.

As I threatened stridently to murder the unknown thief, the boys howled. One leaned toward me and said, "I'd mention it to Laidlaw."

4

I concentrated on the prying aquiline nose and thin-lipped face that was positioned in front of me across the desk. Chief Superintendent Hall had wasted no time in putting his man on the case. Inspector Dennis Robbins was to be in immediate charge of the enquiry and he had hastened to my office.

"I'm going to have to ask you, Nick, whether you know of any place where Sir Robert might have… called in," the Special Branch man said, his voice sardonic, watching me for the slightest sign of evasion. It was an intimate question.

Robbins was in his early thirties, upright and tightly suited in tan gabardine. He gave an impression of precision: groomed dark hair with neat, short barbering; a tightly knotted and centred tie with diagonal stripes of red, gold and black; and a pair of sharp collar points on his white shirt. He had grey eyes, like tiny computer screens, and a faint Australian accent. He was a dedicated career officer and, I thought, not to be treated lightly.

"You mean, a brothel?"

"I'm asking you, Nick. You know what Rawalpindi is like."

"Odd place to start your enquiry, Inspector."

"On the contrary, these are places where a person like Sir Robert would be vulnerable."

"To abduction?"

"Amongst other things."

A man's town; that was how Robert Laidlaw had introduced

'Islamapindi' to me, promising sensual delights beyond my imagination with a crude nudge and wink. Taxi drivers would take me to remote places and rob me; shopkeepers would double their price when they saw me coming; bars would water my drinks; a thief was likely to slip my wallet out of my pocket and the girls would infect me with clap. "But there's great fun to be had! Just got to be a bit wary, Nick."

Robert had cruised the brothels of Karachi, Delhi and Hong Kong as a youth. He knew them as well as any colonial son. I didn't resist his offer to show me the town. The odyssey had started as a tour of sedate hotel lounges– the President, the Marriott and the Sheraton– and then degenerated into an endless series of clubs, topless bars and brothels for a drink and a view of the girls. Naked breasts under blue and red spotlights. At 1am, tired and drunk, we lay in our respective cubicles in a Japanese massage parlour. We were pummelled ineffectually by tiny masseuses.

Later, we recovered in yet another bar, having expensive drinks with girls who knew only a few words of English but had lots of smiles. Robert had rested his back against the bar and glanced around, pleased at the prospect. The sickly flesh of the girls under coloured lights; the shadowy pairs of people huddled in cubicles, engrossed in each other. He had a taste for the seedy. "Do you want a girl, Nick? Some lovely ones here. Select a real beauty."

"Not really," I said. I had no moral objection. I looked at the face of the girl beside me, still as a mask, with ogling eyes. Underneath her transparent dress, I could see the buxom lines of a body that was the colour and heat of milky coffee. On this occasion, though, the idea of acting at Robert's instance jarred me. "No thanks."

"God, where's the old Nick Dyson? You can be a bore at times, Nick."

"Suit yourself. I'll get a cab."

I broke away from Robert's glance, which told me that I was a monster of ingratitude, and went outside. The air was hot and damp and never seemed to fill my lungs. I was in a dark side street. I looked back at a row of black, glistening buildings, which melted together in the moonlight like liquorish. A man sidled up to me, breathing lewdness through broken teeth. He offered a young girl. The secretiveness of the proposal was chilling. He pointed toward the girl. I saw her in the light of a doorway: a slender caramel-coloured child of perhaps ten years, with long hair and bare feet.

"Too young for me, friend," I said, walking out of the alley to hail a cab.

I was beginning to feel imprisoned by the man who faced me. The window behind Robbins was shielded by a white blind, which glared and made my eyes water. I felt I had to give him my attention and that I couldn't get up and draw the curtain. The room was quiet. I tried to take my time under Robbins' eye. It was a matter of breaking an implicit confidence with Robert about private behaviour, but, at the same time, it was also true that any potential clue to his whereabouts that was ignored placed his life in greater danger.

"No, I don't know where Sir Robert might have gone and I doubt if he frequented such places." I was being the protective friend and, possibly, a prude. I knew two places where Robert might have called in, but I felt that Robbins was on the wrong track.

For the sceptical Special Branch officer, whoring was as natural as breathing. "I'll make a few enquiries of my own," he said. "We also have to see anybody here at the High

Commission who might have seen Sir Robert before he left the building."

"What about the police and security people? Shouldn't that be your first stop?"

Robbins jerked his head back. "When I've got hold of what we know here."

When he had gone, I picked up a memo that Rashida had left on my desk. I was summoned to a meeting and lunch at the High Commissioner's Residence, with Bradshaw, Hall, Robbins and Giles Pottinger– the Commission's chief legal officer. The High Commissioner, Sir Hugh Leighton, had been quick to take charge of the event.

The Residence was slightly elevated on a rise beyond the city. It commanded a hazy view over the orange roof tiles, the dark green treetops, and the domes and minarets. The meeting was held in an austere red-draped reception room, which opened out onto the verandah and a flame tree in bloom on the lawn. A water sprinkler made the grass shine and the patter was pleasing.

We quickly settled into capacious chairs around a coffee table with glasses of cold lime juice. A plate of the cookboy's spicy biscuits, fresh from the oven, was placed on the table and we helped ourselves. The biscuits were the subject of some remarks about waistlines.

Leighton stood before us and gestured his satisfaction with the hospitality. The various servants retired. He pushed his fists into the trouser pockets of his cream linen suit and inclined his silver mane. "I'm extremely concerned at the report I've had from you, Leonard. Extremely. However, I don't think we should jump to hasty conclusions. I want everything to remain confidential at this end. Completely confidential. I shall take charge, of course. We should consider this group our action committee until the matter is resolved. And Geoffrey, you'll have to report to London too, but be…"

Robert reported directly to the Prime Minister and the FO in London, and hence his deputy, Geoffrey Bradshaw– or me if necessary– would perform this duty. This independent reporting was an ulcer in the relationship between Robert and Leighton.

"Cautious?" Bradshaw enquired.

"Exactly. Cautious."

"Yes," Bradshaw chuckled. "We don't want to find Robert tomorrow and have London laughing into their sherry about Islamabad having temporarily mislaid a special envoy, do we?"

"Exactly. Perhaps I should report tomorrow…" Leighton mused. "And perhaps you should delay any contact, Geoffrey."

"Excuse me, but how can things remain confidential at this end," I asked, "if Inspector Robbins--"

"Dennis," Leighton smiled.

"If Dennis has to liaise with the police and security?"

"Good point, Nick. I was coming to it myself. We can hold on that for the moment, can't we, Giles?" Leighton asked.

Pottinger suddenly awakened, heavy red eyelids fluttering. "If this is an abduction, it's a crime---"

Hall's dry voice interrupted: "If the police know, the news will be out. Hacks hang around every desk."

"Well, be very discreet, Dennis, and wait a day," Leighton said.

"So, we're not telling London and we're not telling the police either?" I said in astonishment. "How can we get the help we need if we don't tell the police or find out if Pakstani Security have picked up any intelligence?"

Leighton raised his hand to signal a halt to this line of discussion. "We have to be sure of our facts first."

"But how can we find out any facts to be sure of if we don't get help from the police?" I pressed.

Leighton's cheeks swelled with irritation.

Robbins' nasal tones entered the silence. "Nothing at the address I got from a friend of Sir Robert's at the Pakistan Club," he said, turning to me. "The mamma said Laidlaw hadn't been in for weeks. No reason to doubt this."

Leighton frowned. "I hope this isn't going to be a tawdry story." Then, he brightened. "In some ways, though, I suppose that would be simpler for all of us."

His liverish lips contracted with a suppressed amusement that didn't entirely surprise me. I knew Robert had pushed Leighton aside in discussions with the Pakistan Government, failing to inform him about his agenda or the results. When Leighton complained, Robert had told the Foreign Office that he was interfering. Leighton found it hard, even with his cultured veneer, to conceal his dislike. Bradshaw had gossiped to me that Leighton said Robert was a brash ignoramus and a self-seeker. Leighton was off the mark in calling Robert an ignoramus.

"Wife any help?" Bradshaw asked Robbins.

"Last saw him when he left for work yesterday."

"I fear the worst," Hall said, crouching apprehensively over the table.

"I expect we'll soon hear from the abductors, if this is an abduction. They'll want their tuppence worth of recognition," Bradshaw said.

"What a fate that would be!" Leighton said, perhaps mindful of his own vulnerability.

"Robert was pretty much seasoned on the dangers of selling democracy and bargaining for contracts," Bradshaw said, complacently.

"You're being rather cynical, Geoffrey," Leighton said.

"I don't think so. It's the rule they live by, the mullahs and warlords. Lies and double-dealing are daily fare. They'd do to us what we're doing to them. We just have to be aware that it causes animosity, that's all."

"Do we think he could be dead?" Pottinger asked, biting one of the cookies appreciatively. His wiry grey facial hair was like that of a Scottish Terrier.

Pottinger was included in meetings on every subject because of Leighton's anxiety about acting lawfully. Pottinger, for his part, carefully contributed little that was definite– even the self-evident gem about kidnapping being a crime was exceptional. His equivocations were usually quite masterly. In other meetings on other subjects, Bradshaw and I had played the game of *Get Pottinger to Commit Himself*– usually without success. Pottinger fumbled his way through, whatever the subject, anxious to get to the filing cabinet that held his bottle of Johnny Walker by mid afternoon at least.

"Could we work on the basis that both he and Petrie are alive?" I asked.

"I should think that, on balance, they are alive," Hall grated. "If you want to kill a diplomat to make a point, the easiest way to do it is on the spot where you find him. If you go to the trouble of abducting him, then his being alive must be relevant to the point you want to make."

"We'll rest on that hypothesis," Leighton said.

I had become increasingly restless as the talk faffed about with a donnish abstraction – obscuring, rather than exploring, the issue. "Well, what are we going to do?" I asked, after a while.

Hall, the dried-out spy cop, rested his eyes on me as a tenderfoot.

"We need breathing space, another twenty-four hours," Leighton said, irritably.

I could see Leighton preening himself to take over the Kabul talks, which he, as an acknowledged Afghan expert, believed should have been left to him in the first place. Bradshaw, too, was focusing on an enlarged role. Hall was preoccupied with his responsibility and the personal criticism he might face for a grave lapse of security. Only Robbins was a real investigator, but he was a relatively junior one whom I calculated would sit on the sideline and do as he was told.

To me, it was apparent that we were all, except Robbins, above and out of touch with the practicalities of finding a missing person among the hordes in Pakistan. The depressing part was the realisation that there was little we could do except theorise– and it seemed that my colleagues, so far, only wanted to theorise.

I protested, "But Leonard said to me this morning that I should have reported Robert missing last night. I mean, if time is of the essence--"

"Yes," Hall cut in, "an early report may have opened up lines of enquiry."

I thought he was feeling sore; it was likely that a very difficult task was coming his way. I replied sharply, "What practical line of enquiry could have been pursued in the face of this embargo on doing anything?"

Hall shrank back in his chair and directed a mean expression at the coffee table. There was a moment of silence.

"I think that's about enough for now," Leighton said, allowing a good-natured tone of voice to suffuse the gathering. "Can I offer everybody a gin and tonic before lunch?"

5

I changed my mind as my car crawled up the Kashif Gap road that night. I told the driver to go on to the Langar, to the Laidlaw's apartment. I couldn't reach Emma on my mobile, so I decided to call and see her. It took twenty minutes to complete the journey to the tall block that dominated one of the high points of the ridge. It was occasionally mist-bound in the monsoon season, but gave a brilliant view over the lowlands of the Punjab to the south on a clear day, and to the east the white caps of the Himalayas.

If Emma wasn't at home, it wouldn't matter; the drive out of the city was a very pleasant one. I rang the bell on the seventh floor and the housekeeper opened the door. She smiled and bent her head slightly in recognition. "Master," she said. "Lady not home. Go out." There was something sly in her sleek smile that suggested a primed response, but I had to accept it.

"All right, Nadeem, tell Lady Laidlaw I called. Nicholas Dyson."

While I was waiting for the lift, I looked through the windows, along the flank of the Laidlaw apartment. I could see the long patio on that side with its sliding glass doors. On the patio was a figure I recognised, a man who made my chest throb. I moved closer to the window to make sure. The man slipped inside the doors and left the low sun shining on the glass. I was sure, even at that distance, that the man was Gerald Macbeth– the lean figure, the dark waves of hair and the cat-like movement.

I descended in the lift and walked out of the lobby entrance to look for my driver. My car– a standard, black, High Commission Ford saloon– was parked at the kerb 30 yards away. Beyond it was a golden Bentley Turbo. A uniformed chaffeur was polishing it proudly. The two drivers were talking, but parted when they saw me.

"Whose car is that?" I asked, as I slid into the back seat of the Ford.

The driver grinned, "Boss Macbeth. Very rich!"

I stretched in my seat, sweating uncomfortably as the driver moved the car carefully away. The chance that Macbeth would cross my path– or for that matter Robert's and Emma's as well– was one of my concerns when Robert had first approached me to join him. At one point, I had even tried to talk Robert out of going to Pakistan himself. 'It's a very dangerous appointment. And how can you be a leading member of a foreign community– really a relatively small community– with that man who hates you?' I asked him. Robert had pretended not to understand. 'You're talking rubbish. This is the opportunity of a lifetime! Stop feeling so guilty, Nick.'

I didn't feel guilty. I was apprehensive. I felt that the past should be allowed to rest and that nothing should be done to disturb it. In London, in the face of Robert's certitude, I had begun to believe that I was being over-cautious, even a bit neurotic. However my fears were reawakened when I discovered what a shadow the Macbeth Docks & Trading Company cast over Pakistan. It was one of the big enterprises that underpinned the economy, with a history going back to the nineteenth century. At its heart was Gerald Macbeth. We– Robert, Emma and I– had walked freely into his lair. I grasped the back of the front seat with both hands to suppress my agitation.

Over the years since I had left Poole Abbey, I thought a lot about going back to the prize-giving at the end of the summer term. 'Commem', as it was called, was two days of sports, displays of work, receptions, parties, speeches and meetings of 'old boys'. When I was a schoolboy, I used to imagine what it would be like to be an old boy and return. I would have a superb sports car. I would be a wealthy celebrity, drink sherry with Larsen's successor and sit at one of the specially reserved seats at the front of the marquee. If I was particularly distinguished, my dreams placed me on the platform in the assembly hall during the presentation of prizes by the Head. And the vision continued when I left Poole Abbey, year after year, reeling over and over in my mind, and becoming– like an old, worn, black-and-white film– more and more surreal.

When I was working in London, it took me a long time to summon up the determination to go back to the school– not that I was ashamed of what I had achieved as a barrister, little as it was. I could hold my own with the other loudmouths and there was nobody I was afraid to look in the eye, but I knew that my peers' success stories would be like needles pricking my ears. I usually consulted the *Poole Abbey Old Boys Magazine*, noted the Commem dates and then did nothing. On one occasion, I went as far as filling in the attendance forms and sending them off. I could feel the weight of my inertia, which increased as the date approached, turning almost to repulsion. I cancelled, yet remained desperate, absurdly, to glimpse the past. So, with each year that passed, it became the thing I had to do.

One summer, after I had been at the bar for four years,

I put off my cases, packed clothes for three days– creams for cricket, swimming trunks, squash and tennis rackets, and my dinner jacket– and got behind the wheel of the second-hand BMW drop-head sports that I had just about bankrupted myself to buy. I had a booking at The White Swan at the edge of Sherborne town with a pleasant room that looked out onto a stream and grazing fields.

After so many years I expected the town and the school to have changed, but they hadn't. It was like looking at an old photograph, slightly faded. I strolled around. The neat, golden-cream sandstone houses were graying. The conservative, dark green paint on some shop fronts had dulled, but the boys looked the same in their crumpled grey uniforms, with pale faces and golden hair. The imposing eighteenth-century quadrangle of the school itself, surrounded by buildings with battlements and towers, was precisely intact. This might have been any prize-giving at the end of any summer term in the last twenty or thirty years or more. I felt like a spirit rather than a connected person as I mingled with the boys and the guests.

The celebrations started with a reception at March House on a sultry Dorset afternoon, the air weighted with hay dust and pollen and the scent of honeysuckle. The lawn behind March House was burnt by the sun. Trestle tables were covered with white cloths. The men's foreheads were red in the heat. The women sheltered under broad-brimmed straw hats with bright bands. Salad and cream sponge were served and bottles of champagne rested in ice buckets on the tables.

I didn't know the new housemaster or any of his staff, nor did I recognise any of the old boys or parents at this gathering. I was indisputably entitled to be part of the scene and yet I was a stranger. I stood in a group of guests without conversing, though the experience of my years at March and the Abbey was sufficient to enable me to talk confidently if I chose.

I looked up in the hazy air at the colonnaded outline of the building, built and endowed by Sir Joseph March, a wealthy merchant who ran clipper ships to the China coast in the 1850s. March House was a product of the opium trade. And it was in this garden, in the shadow of the beech trees at the end of the lawn, that I had heard the scream...

I looked down. At one of the tables near me, some of the senior boys were sipping champagne. March always had a liberal attitude to champagne and strawberries at Commem. The boys had passed the giggling stage and were now groaning with suppressed laughter. They were beginning to attract sidelong glances. I was watching them, amused, remembering my Commems as a student. I felt the intense sun rays on my head. A woman leaned toward me, a scraggy, long-haired blonde with leathery skin, and said, "If you were at March House, Mr Dyson, you must have been here at the time of the scandal."

"What scandal?" the man beside me demanded, surging out of lethargy.

"About a boy named Gerald Macbeth, don't you remember?" the woman said, waving her red claws in my face.

"What, from the Karachi family?" the man pressed.

The past was seeping into the heavy air. Without answering, I suddenly excused myself, replaced my glass on the table and walked into the shadow of the cloisters. The red lips of the boys, stained with strawberry juice, were printed on my mind like a design on a screen. I passed quickly into the coolness of the corridors of the house. On impulse I left the building by the front door, walked up the rise to The Swan, packed my bags and checked out. On the drive back to London, I felt that I had avoided a stifling and depressing cloud.

When I returned to my apartment, I phoned Emma Laidlaw. "I called in at your place a while ago but you were out, apparently."

"Yes, Nick," Emma said, blandly. "What did you want?" Emma could be chilly.

"To tell you the latest on the search for Robert. What else?" Actually, there was a hell of a lot of 'else'. I wanted to see and be with her for a while. I wanted to find out if she ever thought about us.

"Well?" she said.

I told her that Robert hadn't been found and that Leighton was reporting later to the Foreign Office.

"I know. Hugh Leighton called me."

"You don't seem too concerned."

"Robert's probably gone off with his Pakistani mistress. That's what I told the police. I assume that awful prat Robbins is a policeman of some kind. He went through all of Robert's private papers here. When I asked, 'What's that got to do with finding Robert?' he said, 'Don't you want to cooperate in finding your husband?' He said he was looking for names of people who might know something. He even wanted to know if Robert had a foreign bank account– not just his old London one or his local one. I told him Robert didn't have any bloody money, so why would he have a foreign bank account?"

It didn't sound right. Robbins seemed to be on a different track. "I don't know why Robbins would ask about bank accounts. You should have called me, Emma, before you let him look at Robert's papers."

Actually, I knew why he might ask about a foreign bank

account, but it seemed to me to be an enquiry that had nothing to do with Robert's disappearance. Certainly, an impertinence.

I didn't believe that Robert had any sort of a mistress as Emma had suggested – at least, not somebody he saw regularly. We shared this sort of confidence, although he never talked about Emma. Emma was a black hole in our relationship. I wasn't clear how much Robert knew about my past association with Emma, but he certainly knew something.

"Never mind. Robert's indestructible. He'll turn up," she said, perkily.

When I put the phone down, I cursed myself for being too cowardly to mention that I had seen Macbeth– that was really why I'd called her, to tell her, to ask her… Hell, what was she doing with the man? I needed to explain to her that she could be putting herself in danger. Or was that being over-dramatic? Or jealous? That was how it would look to Emma. I had a drink and took time to think about ringing her back, then I had another drink and another. Scotch. I was burning inside about what was going on in that apartment at the Langar. How Macbeth was there when Robert had hardly gone out of the door!

After a while, I couldn't see straight enough to dial the number. Ashraf's tasty tandoori turkey with rice congealed in its bowl on the dining room table.

6

The next morning I arrived at my office at 10am, pale-faced, with a hangover. I had hardly seated myself at my desk before I received a call from Robbins.

"I'm at the Sheraton Hotel," he said in a rasping official voice that emphasised his squashed vowels. "I'd like you to come over immediately."

I don't respond very well to orders, but my first thought was the possibly beneficial effect of a visit to the Pilot's Bar at the Sheraton for a Bloody Mary. "What's up?"

"You may be able to help. It's about Petrie."

"What about him?" I wasn't sure whether it was the queasiness of my stomach or Robbins' mechanical tone that made me feel uneasy. I hadn't the energy to question him and a stroll was welcome– anything but being stared at by a computer screen.

"I'd prefer it if you came over," Robbins declared flatly.

"OK, I won't be long."

It was a short walk down Habib Path in the breathless humidity from the government offices to the Chundrigar commercial centre, then across a paved area of sapling trees, palms and a fountain to the hotel entrance. A uniformed Pakistani police officer who worked in liaison with Robbins recognised me and intercepted me on the front steps.

"If you'll come with me to the tenth floor, please, sir."

I was going to ask him what was happening, but the man looked through me and volunteered nothing. When we arrived at the floor, the hall was cordoned off and numerous uniformed and plain-clothes cops were talking quietly in groups. I felt ill. I knew something grim had happened. The horror was palpable in the stiff faces of the talkers.

Robbins came forward, unsmiling, and pointed down the hall. "I want you to take a look at this. Follow me."

He made no attempt to prepare me for what I was about to see. A cruel spot in him was pleased to see my loss of composure. He led me into suite 1062. The elegant room, with its thick carpets, soft green and gold colourings and pale satin drapes, seemed to have received the attention of a crazy painter. The walls were splashed in stark patterns. Blood. A raw stench packed the air. The bed was saturated.

At one side of the room, resting on a sheet of plastic, a shape, roughly the shape of a man, was draped in another sheet of plastic. I put a hand over my nose to block the sickening smell. Robbins jerked the cover away from the form. A headless corpse was revealed, wearing a once-white, short-sleeved shirt and a dark blue tie that ineffectually circled the stump of its neck.

"Where's the head?" How I managed to ask this question, I don't know. I was struggling against a faint.

"Can you identify?" Robbins asked.

"It looks like Petrie. No watch, though. He had a gold Rolex."

"They wouldn't leave that. What about this stuff?" He pointed to a dark jacket that was draped over a side table. A cream straw hat was perched on top, with the red, green and blue band of Petrie's former Black Watch regiment.

"The hat looks like his. Do you have any idea what happened?" I said, trying to keep the vomit from rising in my throat. I thought I was going to make a fool of myself in front of Robbins.

Robbins looked chastened, but very much in control. "When the body was found, the headless corpse was sitting up on the bed with banners across the bed-head. It looks as though the performance was filmed. An execution. No sign of the head, but it will turn up somewhere, sometime."

"What do the banners say?" The white-lettered black material was folded in a pile on the carpet.

"Death to the infidel who insults Allah, or to that effect."

The photographers were folding up their cameras and tripods. The forensic technicians had completed their examination and the results were packed in containers by the door. I thought of the Lancashire woman, waiting.

"Does Mrs Petrie know?" I asked.

"I'll be seeing her when I leave here. It's Mrs Burns actually. I may want to speak to you when I get through here. Why don't you wait downstairs in the bar?"

I could not have been dismissed with a more sensible suggestion. I went down to the Pilot's Bar and had a double whisky and soda. A Bloody Mary would have been a gentle return to sanity. I needed something more toxic. It was twenty minutes before Robbins joined me, glad to break a rule and accept a drink on duty. I was on my second.

"Isn't this a kind of overkill?" I asked.

"Not if you want to terrify people."

"This isn't going to look good in the papers. You won't be able to keep Robert's disappearance quiet any longer."

"We can put a security blanket over the whole thing for a while here. This isn't like Britain. However, the FO are more concerned about the British media's reaction if there's too much delay. You know, a day's silence and it's a cover-up. London are scared of the media. They've told us to release the news."

"Then the pressure will really be on Hall– and you– to

get some results. Are you likely to be flooded with help from the Metropolitan Police in London?"

"I expect some of them might fancy an exotic holiday. But no cop from London can really help unless he's fluent in the native lingos."

"Do you have any leads on Robert from upstairs?"

"The forensics may turn up something. The room was reserved for Sir Robert. Staff say he was here at about 3pm on the day he disappeared and there were visitors. Some kind of meeting."

"Who booked the room?"

"The reception staff say they understood it was the High Commission, but there's no record."

"Wouldn't the hotel want a credit card?"

"Not from the High Commission, apparently. I'll try to find out who made the booking. It's an important point. The booking was for two nights. And I don't expect there was any reason why Sir Robert would take a room for himself for that length of time. For one night, perhaps, to have a meeting, but not two. The booking was probably made by the person who wanted to lure him into a trap. Did you know anything about a meeting?"

"No."

"Isn't that strange? I mean, you were, in effect, shadowing him."

"Robert was hard to keep up with."

"I'd like to know more about the people you and he were meeting."

"If Robert and Petrie were here on the day they disappeared, why didn't room service discover Petrie yesterday?"

"There was a 'Do not disturb' notice on the door and room service had been told their services weren't required yesterday. They do what they're told here without too many questions. Now, about the people you've been meeting."

"I assume you're getting information from the FO team. We generate enough damn paper and emails on everything we do."

"Yes, but I'd like to hear from you personally. You were closest to Sir Robert."

"In Kabul, we met mostly government officials. We had a rather passing contact with others at a reception and dinner, and we stayed overnight at the Embassy. Robert had meetings with officials and contractors seeking contracts."

"Minuted meetings?"

"No. Too unimportant, I suppose."

"Unimportant, seriously? Regarding contracts that may have been for millions of dollars?" Robbins sat up straight and sounded sceptical.

"I mean, no progress. No decisions. Just talk."

"Why weren't you a party to these meetings?"

"If Robert wanted to act alone, he did."

"Were Pakistanis involved? Americans?"

"Some. Well, you know a lot of interests are involved in the way Afghanistan is set up or when it concerns a slice of the contracts for reconstruction and arms. It's pigs' snouts in the trough. I'll let you have the names I know, but I can't see how this can solve our problem."

"Good. I'll have everybody screened. Any inducements offered for contracts?"

"A little money to grease the palm is probably always on offer, but we don't do business that way."

"How do you know Sir Robert didn't?"

"Because he's an honest man and wouldn't jeopardise his career. It's not a very helpful question."

"I have to explore every possible motivation. Suppose Sir Robert had disappointed a paymaster?"

"That's preposterous."

"No threats of violence against Sir Robert?"

"No, other than the overarching security problem. Petrie is dead upstairs and you seem more interested in ridiculous suggestions of corrupt practice by the man he was hired to protect."

Robbins could see that I had lost patience with his line of questioning. He lowered his eyes, tossed down the remainder of his drink and left the bar.

I rang Emma and told her in as guarded language as I could that Petrie had been murdered and that there was no sign of Robert. "We must hope that we can catch up with the people who took Robert while he's still OK. I mean, it's awful to say it, but in a way it gives us hope that we haven't found him. It could mean he's still alive."

Emma listened to me in silence, and then said, "So it really is the most terrible trouble and not just Robert goofing off on another damn silly adventure."

She seemed to believe it for the first time.

"It's real, Emma."

I wanted to say I'd get in my car and come to see her immediately, but it wasn't necessary. She was calm. I thought that her words of sympathy about Petrie seemed superficial. Her occasional remoteness and her unexpected reactions were part of the attraction for me.

I walked disconsolately back to the office and had a long session explaining the details to Bradshaw, who received them enigmatically, making notes. I spent the rest of the day sat in my room, the computer screen blank, a piled of unread papers in front of me, shocked, not thinking clearly. The memory of the blood-spattered walls and the charnel house smell would take time to recede, as would the memory of Petrie, who was never a friend, but at least a vibrant and pleasant physical presence in the office. Late in the afternoon, I made a painful, inarticulate telephone call to Petrie's partner.

7

The next day I worked like an automaton, not daring to think outside the requirements of my computer screen. I left the office early. Leighton and his supervisory group surprisingly didn't surface– I couldn't imagine why, in the aftermath of such an event. I would have to visit Petrie's partner, but at the moment I felt cowed.

Instead of going directly home by car, I decided to walk in the city. I asked my driver to wait at the High Commission. I had no destination. I merely wanted to have people moving around me. The air was cloyingly soft; the haze overhead, yellow. I sauntered under the palms. I listened to the splutter of a fountain, which seemed to become deafeningly loud. On Khaled Square, I saw an English language newspaper billboard at a vendor's stand: British Envoy Missing – Aide hacked to death.

I bought a copy of the newspaper, *The Karachi Evening News*, and went to the haunt of expatriates, the Press Club at the Hilton. With a bottle of Budweiser, I settled on a stool at the bar. The story in the newspaper was short, muddled and based on speculation. The hacks had been caught napping and could only dig around in their old files for padding.

I tested the story against my own threadbare knowledge. As Robert's assistant, I had complete access to his files except the Top Secret ones– that murky pool of political sensitivities, proposals and initiatives was entirely unknown to me. When I had asked that I be cleared for Top Secret access, Robert and

Bradshaw had both told me that the files contained a lot of irrelevant rubbish as far as my job was concerned. 'Canteen regulations, circa 1910,' Bradshaw had said. Still, they had carefully blocked my access to the files in lieu of a clearance and I was too proud to make an issue of it.

I was beginning to realise how little I knew and therefore how amateurish my speculation might be. I was even beginning to suspect that I was not really privy to the information received by Leighton's steering committee. They invited me to meetings, but perhaps they conferred without me. Paranoia? Cynicism, certainly.

As *The Evening News* pointed out, acts of terrorism and murder had already been committed against British expatriates, so terrorism against the British presence with Robert as a symbol seemed not unlikely. But did that square with abduction? Yes, it would be a way of dragging out the pain– impossible ransom demands making ultimate recovery of a corpse more inevitable and shocking. The British, the American and their Pakistani allies could never yield to the likely call for withdrawal of troops– that call would amount to no more than a deathly wail. But the release of prisoners which was, on the face of it, rejected as a ransom demand– was something that depended on the importance of the prisoners concerned on both sides. This was where abduction could possibly be used by the Taliban and jihadists as a tool.

Al Jesira television had already broadcast images of captives awaiting execution.

It would be horrifying if Robert's final appearance on world television was in an orange suit with a hooded executioner. Perhaps, in advance of that, a video of Petrie's execution would also appear.

In the meantime, I believed we should be making

extreme efforts to locate Robert. If he was going to be found, it could only be done by sound Pakistani detective work on the ground, boosted with a little luck or a tip-off. However assiduous Robbins might be, he could not personally provide this. I didn't think that the abduction could be anything more than a political act. Petrie's execution appeared to confirm that the killers wished to make a crude political statement. I couldn't seriously believe the line of enquiry, which Robbins seemed so anxious to pursue, about unrequited bribes leading to a reprisal.

I had a natural reluctance to think that Gerald Macbeth, the scion of a wealthy and long-established family, could be involved in anything so vile as this, although there was a kind of indirect present connection with Robert. Macbeth Docks was one of the big construction companies seeking reinstatement contracts.

I had never mentioned Macbeth to Robbins – the relationship was too complicated. Nor had I said anything of the note to a woman in Robert's desk drawer (which I had appropriated to avoid his embarrassment). There was nothing that I had ever seen in Robert's papers that would give a clue to his disappearance. Rashida had implied that Robert left the office in the company of a woman, probably the 'C' in his note.

It occurred to me that Robbins would not rest with information gained from Robert's papers, from Bradshaw and from me. He had already been to Robert's apartment and searched his desk. He might ask to make a more thorough examination of the files in Robert's office. I was fairly familiar with them. In my opinion, this would be a waste of his time.

I began to think what other papers Robert might have. Robbins seemed so set on an enquiry into the possibility of bribery, rather than following up what happened at the Sheraton, that it was beginning to alarm and anger me. There was one other place that would probably be searched: a safe that Robert sometimes used as a storeroom at the High Commission. I had the combination because I also used it on rare occasions.

I paused over my drink. Robbins didn't dream up the idea of bribery on his own. He must have received a complaint. I would find out about that. For the moment, concerned that the investigation into Robert's disappearance had veered off course, I decided that I should have a look at the safe myself.

I walked slowly back to the offices of the High Commission to avoid breaking into a sweat. The security officers at the entrance were part of the night shift and didn't recognise me. I showed my pass and signed in. The place was empty apart from a few cleaners. Not many of the civil servants worked late. I used the lift to get to the little-used top floor of the building, where the walk-in safe was off a dark hall. Using the key and combination, I opened the door and stepped inside.

Most of the shelves were unused. A nearly empty gin bottle and a full bottle of cognac were relics of an office party. One shelf had a tray of cardboard-covered folders and a box of voice tapes from past meetings. I flicked through this material, which was more or less familiar to me— or so old that it couldn't be relevant.

Under a lower shelf at the back was a bulky parcel in plastic wrapping. I pulled the wrapping away to reveal a blue canvas sports bag, big enough to hold tennis rackets, sports clothes and towels. I dragged the bag out; it was heavy, bulked out with something other than sports gear. I unzipped the opening.

A rank smell pricked my nostrils. I disturbed the wrapping paper. Delicate green patterns shimmered under the weak electric light in the safe. The bag was stuffed with United States dollars, packets and packets of used one hundred dollar bills. I swayed over the hoard for a moment, bemused. Then I pushed my fingers into the pile, pulled out two or three packets, sniffed them absently and let them drop back into the bag. I had no idea of the total value of the money, but it was a huge sum. What was Robert doing with such a sum? He was always complaining about poverty and his expense account drove the Foreign Office wild. In my hasty examination of the bag, I could find no accompanying address label or note.

This find could be damning for Robert, although there were possible explanations. I decided to remove the bag until I understood a little more of its provenance. I didn't stop to appreciate the risk I was taking. I zipped up the bag, hefted it over my shoulder, closed the safe and rang my driver on the way down to the front door. I signed out under the eye of the guards with a polite nod and a smile, and walked away with the strap of the overstuffed bag nearly breaking my shoulder. I swung the weight slightly– a civil servant heading for the gym.

My driver was waiting with the car at the front door. I rested the bag on the back seat beside me and wiped the moisture from my forehead and palms. We were quickly through the security barriers and on the way to my apartment. I felt elated, which I quickly realised was a perverse reaction. The money wasn't mine and I was taking a huge gamble to protect Robert.

After dinner that night and after Ashraf had retired, I counted the money on the dining table: One million two hundred thousand American dollars, all in packets of one hundred dollar bills. The money was divided into three packages, each wrapped in different plain paper. The way the bills were bundled suggested one source. No other paper in the bag gave a clue to the origin of the money. The bag was made in Karachi and had the sports firm label 'Wilson.' It could well have belonged to Robert, who was a very competent tennis player.

I sat at the dining room table with the packets of bills piled before me. The sheer quantity gave me an uneasy thrill. I had never seen so much, even in a casino. I tried to work out where Robert could have got it. He loved politics, but he always said a poor politician was open to corruption. Of course, there were a number of people who would gladly have paid for his favour – and, in the solitary way he worked, I couldn't be absolutely sure of his integrity. He often joked with me about bribes and kick-backs, because we were being offered them at times. He always took care to say he would share the proceeds with me. I took this as a joke. He would pad his expenses or relieve the cash box of a few dollars, yes, but these were open excesses. He was honest as far as I knew in monetary matters– sexually duplicitous, but financially honest.

I was also sure that Robert knew very well that his prospects for honour and wealth, were so bright that it would be senseless to jeopardise them. However, even people who are stars do senseless things at times, which involve risking their own reputation and future. The Robert I knew would be capable of taking a risk with his reputation, daring the world to bring him down. Even so, I couldn't bring myself to believe he had done so here.

Whatever the complexities of his personality, there was another far simpler possibility. The money could be a donation to party political funds– no doubt made by a donor with an ulterior objective, but nevertheless lawful and temporarily resting in the safe on its way to party HQ in London. That was a real possibility. But why so much, and why in cash? I supposed that the answer was that there are very rich people in the East who seek advantage and are prepared to pay for it.

At that moment, the doorbell rang. I heard Ashraf emerge from his room near the front door. I stuffed as many of the packets back into the bag as I could and swept the rest onto the floor, pushing them across the polished woodblock surface behind a screen where I also dropped the bag. Ashraf advanced into the room, closely followed by Emma Laidlaw, who obviously did not regard herself as being required to wait at the door.

"Master…?" Ashraf said, apologetically.

"It's all right, Ashraf. You go," I said.

"You call on me, Nick. I call on you," Emma said, poised in her tight purple T-shirt and equally tight thigh–length white shorts.

I tried to cover my confusion with hospitable suavity. "Emma! Come out onto the terrace. I'll get you a drink."

Emma walked up to me and when I bent to kiss her cheek, she offered her lips instead and pressed the length of her body against me. I couldn't resist letting my palms stray across her back.

She pressed me away with a snigger. "Darling, what's that funny smell?"

I could smell it, too. My hands. The money. The dirty–fingered stink of used paper money. "Oh, sorry. I was cleaning out some old books in the spare room. I'll go and wash my hands."

Emma was reclining on one of the terrace chairs when

I came back. Ashraf had placed two lamps outside to smoke the insects away. I opened the glass doors to their widest, so that I could talk to Emma from the lounge while I mixed the dry martinis we had agreed. I didn't want her wandering around the room. While Ashraf could serve us both gin and tonics, a dry martini was beyond him.

"Nick, you don't know how worried I've been since Petrie's murder. I can't believe that, or something like it, has happened to Robert…"

As we sipped our martinis, the talk of Robert died away. It was twilight, with the blue lawns below, the scent of flowers, the roaring of the cicadas in the bush-covered hills and the last red flare of the sun on the distant mountain peaks.

The thought that Gerald Macbeth had been with Emma gave me a nauseous feeling. I wasn't sure how to approach the subject with her.

I had known Emma since I was at school. I had lost track of her afterwards but I never forgot her. After I had settled myself with a pupillage in the chambers of a leading criminal silk in London, I set out to find her. I rang her mother in Dorset and gave her a story about being a long-lost friend. I learned Emma had joined a publishing company in Fleet Street, then a public relations firm and finally an art gallery. When I walked into the gallery in Cork Street where she worked, in my dark blue chalk-striped suit and waistcoat, with a Hermes tie of quiet brilliance, I hoped to be the kind of attractive and prosperous man that any young female gallery attendant would be pleased to see– customer or not. Emma Southern, as she then was, didn't recognise me!

No doubt I'd changed. I'd spent a number of undistinguished years at Swansea University getting my law degree and another eighteen months of travelling in the United States (working in bars and back-packing), and then I'd passed my bar exams. I had completely overestimated my importance as a figure in Emma's past.

She was embarrassed but not displeased when I introduced myself. Seeing her clouded eyes, I quickly mentioned Poole Abbey. She seemed to be as fresh and exciting as I remembered her. She had hardly changed. I sat confidently on the edge of her vast desk, but I didn't feel confident at all. She looked round at her colleagues to see whether they could hear the conversation and seemed to be relieved that they couldn't.

"Nicholas Dyson," she repeated slowly, her tongue exploring the syllables. "That's a very long time ago. And, of course, I remember you… and everything."

I sensed that she was pleased at the approach of a presentable man, but discomforted by a past she wanted to forget. She refused to go out for a coffee then, but reluctantly accepted an invitation to lunch, which would be arranged in a phone call a day or two later.

I took her to the Tate Gallery restaurant on the Embankment and as soon as we had settled down facing each other, sipping red wine, oblivious of the other diners around, the question came: "Do you ever see Bob Laidlaw, Nick?"

I knew Robert would come into the conversation and I hated it, but it was a connection with Emma. "Sure, we've kept in touch, mostly postcards, but in touch. He's down from Cambridge now with an investment bank in the City. Very involved in politics."

"So he got to Cambridge…"

"That touch of excellence, you know." I was unable to conceal the note of sourness.

She looked at me sharply, then smiled slightly. "Do we love him or do we hate him?" she asked, impulsively covering my hand, resting on the table, with her own.

My attachment to Emma started at Poole Abbey, but this was the moment when an attachment started between us both.

Now, sitting on the terrace in the soft light, Emma was my particular vision of beauty and desirability. She was a virus in my blood. It was quite irrational. She was not a particularly well-educated woman. She had had a rudimentary college education at an indulgent girls' boarding school, which she had abandoned at sixteen. She was shrewd rather than clever. Her middle-class background gave her social poise. She had energy and verve, but no reserves of insight that I had ever discovered. And yet, above all other women that I had met, she had the effect of casting me into a whirlwind of hopes and dreams.

How her ephemeral qualities could cause such a fever, I couldn't understand. It was the way she angled her chin, the way her dark hair curled over her forehead, the squirm of her lips, the enticing dark blue eyes. I had enjoyed other women, whose qualities of body or mind outmatched Emma's, but none had her indefinable attraction.

The thought of Gerald Macbeth close to her stuck in my throat like a lump of Ashraf's steak. "I saw Macbeth's car outside your apartment when I was there."

"Whose?"

"Oh, come on, Emma, don't bullshit."

She turned her head toward me, levelling with my eyes. "So, you saw his car. Maybe he has a lover there. Fifteen levels, fifty-nine apartments not counting ours. Plenty of choice," she smiled, cruelly.

I sighed. "If you get involved with Macbeth, I don't know what will happen."

A long pause followed and then she said, "I owe him something."

"You can't pay, even if you do."

"I do owe him," she said, emphatically.

"Emma, don't be a fool. You can't make up for what happened at Poole Abbey. It's past. Over. You have to go on in a different direction." I leaned over and kissed her on the neck without knowing quite what to expect from her.

She shivered pleasurably and smothered my lips with her mouth and tongue. "Let's make love, Nick, like we used to. Let's make love here, now, now…"

8

Emma stayed with me that night. I had been overcome by her impetuosity. At one moment I was in an agony of jealousy over Macbeth and in the next, surging with passion for her, sprawling over her body on the couch in the moonlight— both of us too excited to spare the time to undress completely. It was always the same. When Emma made love, it wasn't a giving on her side. It was a forgetting, as though she was taking a drug. Emma was a taker. I couldn't possess her. I could only watch her ecstasy— although, to be fair, I enjoyed myself.

The next morning I took an early phone call from the High Commissioner in my office, the scent of Emma still pervading my senses despite a shower and a complete change of clothing. I sipped strong black coffee and tried to concentrate on Leighton's words.

"The FO have decided that we should keep to the schedule for the talks, Nick. Whatever the cause of Laidlaw's disappearance, they're determined to press on. They've already sent somebody else out to take over."

Leighton's habitual urbanity could not conceal tones of astonishment and regret, which he would not particularly want to communicate to me. I wasn't sufficiently interested in Foreign Office affairs to ask who the newcomer was. I was more interested in myself. "Where does this leave me, Hugh?"

"Carry on regardless. There's not going to be any public

announcement of a replacement, not at this stage. The FO will wait and see what happens. I want you to come up to the Residence at 10.30am for an introduction."

I asked the driver to let me out a few hundred yards short of the Residence. I walked slowly up the rise, with my jacket over my shoulder. The city traffic grinded under a pall of blue fumes in the distance. I kept in the shade of the avenue of plane trees. My head was clearing and my natural optimism was returning.

In my sessions with Emma, it was always sex first, then boozing into insensibility. I had no guilt about my association with her. The reverse. Emma's occasional acts of adultery with me (and perhaps others) was a price Robert had to pay. As a result of my experience in the past with both of them, I felt I had as much right to Emma as he had. I had a slight sense of discomfort that others in the diplomatic community might know of our attachment and I would appear to be disloyal and callous, but I wasn't in a position to explain.

When I arrived at the portico of the Residence and passed through the security guards, I slipped into my jacket and was shown into one of the shaded reception rooms. Half a dozen people were already gathered together. Only a few were familiar faces. My shirt stuck coldly to my skin in the air-conditioned room.

Sir Hugh Leighton took me by the arm and brought me into the main group. "I want you to meet Robert Laidlaw's personal assistant, Nicholas Dyson, Grace. This is the man who will be your right hand," he said, turning to me. "Grace Stewart."

I shook hands with a small, slender woman of thirty something, perhaps forty, with short fair hair and hazel eyes. In a grey cotton costume, a white blouse and with a calculating composure, I thought she looked much more like a future ambassador than Bradshaw. He was now at her elbow wearing a clownish smile. I chatted to her briefly in a moment when she was alone. She was solicitous about Robert and, in her Edinburgh accent, she told me how much she was depending on me. She seemed very modest.

It was Bradshaw who later filled in the details about her, as though he had memorised her curriculum vitae. "She's rather able, I'm afraid," he said, as though this was a disability. We were together at the edge of the gathering, which had now swelled to more than a dozen. "Graduate of Edinburgh in modern languages, distinguished civil service entrance marks, School of Oriental Studies, Beijing, Delhi. All that stuff. Very competent and she's a woman– as far as we know– which gives her a head start!"

Bradshaw's frivolity had a tinny edge. It was not enough to cloak his disappointment.

Leighton withdrew me from Bradshaw in his practiced way and steered me toward a new pair. "Nick, this is Howard Chunagar of the Karachi city council."

"We've met," I said, and took the hand of the gracious, elderly Anglo-Pakistani barrister.

"And Gerald Macbeth, Pakistani Businessmen's Association."

"Hullo, Macbeth," I said, not extending my hand, knowing instinctively that the young man with the dark, cavern-eyed stare would ignore me.

Macbeth did not reply. He deliberately turned away. Leighton's attention had flitted elsewhere. He missed the snub.

Bradshaw caught me as I backed away. "What did you think of our merchant prince?" he asked in a confidential whisper.

"Nothing," I said, wrestling with a feeling of annoyance and ill-will.

"Oh dear. You haven't been properly briefed."

"I know who he is," I said, tersely.

"Not enough, dear boy. The son of the deceased Iron Mick, head of Macbeth Docks & Trading. Owns a sizable slice of the economy. Oh, yes. He doesn't trust us."

"You mean Leighton?"

"I mean our gracious sovereign's government, the old firm that has supported his family's efforts since 1850."

"Really?" I said in a chilly voice, unable not to look in Macbeth's direction. Macbeth would not allow himself a second glance in mine. Here was the man whom I saw as a black spider at the centre of the web that entangled Robert, Emma and me. And there was something spiderish about him and threateningly dark. At the same time, the people around him were listening to his commanding tones.

"You'll have to convince him, Nick, that we Brits are only selling the same old codswallop that we peddled over 150 years ago. New packaging, of course. No flags and red coloured maps this time, but tame and feeble democracies leaning on us for arms, oil sales and mighty engineering works."

"I know Chunagar and Macbeth are lobbyists. I've dealt with Chunagar." I snapped out the words. In the hustle, Bradshaw did not notice my manner.

"Don't underestimate them. They're not the Little Puddlington parish council, you know. Beware!" Bradshaw said, looking at me archly, trying to convey a number of septic significances on his pudgy face. Then, his expression changed. "I say, my boy, you don't look at all well."

As I was leaving the room, Superintendent Hall asked me to stay for a meeting of 'our committee'. "I want Dennis to bring us up to date," he said. He hinted with a slight lift of his lizard-like eyelids that there was progress to report.

I waited for five minutes outside the reception room while the meeting with Grace Stewart ended. I didn't want to be in the reception while Macbeth was present.

Robbins was waiting too, but it was easy to avoid conversation in the shady hall with others coming and going. We were ushered into the white lounge with Leighton, Pottinger, Bradshaw, Grace Stewart and Hall. When we were seated comfortably and the house boy had served coffee, Leighton took the floor and welcomed Grace Stewart. He looked grim; his summer suit seemed yellowed, almost stained, against the brightness of the room.

"We've had the expected contact from Laidlaw's abductors, a group associated with Al Qaeda who call themselves the Independence Faction. This is going to cause very serious political problems for all of us." He paused, his eyes fluttering up toward the ornate cornice edging in the ceiling.

"What about Robert?" I interjected.

"And, of course, it's very worrying as far as Laidlaw's safety is concerned," Leighton added hurriedly, frowning at me. He nodded to Robbins.

Robbins smoothed his fingers along the sharp crease in his trousers, preparing with relish to occupy centre stage. "I have a note," he said, opening a file cover to show a page of characters written in black ink and surrounded by a black border. "It was handed in by a messenger at the Rawalpindi City Central police station this morning. It demands immediate withdrawal of British and American troops from Iraq and Afghanistan to enable local democracy to flourish, and promises extermination of Anglo-American capitalist lackeys in default."

"The usual," Leighton said.

"What about Robert?" I asked, again.

"He's not mentioned. Al Qaeda sometimes operate in an elliptical way," Robbins said.

"Rather an incongruous method to achieve 'local democracy'," Pottinger sniffed.

"By murder and terrorism, you mean?" Bradshaw smiled, smugly. "I thought that was perfectly normal. Britain, France and Israel, to name but three."

"We know this group," Hall interjected loudly, glowering at the byplay. "We should be able to get a line on them. Three of them have served time here and in India for political offences. They've been active in Kabul and Bagdad, but haven't extended violence to Pakistan before."

"I hope you're able to push the investigation forward," Grace Stewart said quietly, "because there's a very critical media out there. This thing could turn into a nail-biting international scandal if we don't run it down quickly."

"It's not a thing," I said. "It's a search for a man in danger of his life."

"Of course, that's what Grace meant, I'm sure…" Leighton puffed.

"Marvellous copy," Bradshaw sighed. "Violent murder. Diplomatic missions. Abduction. Every muckraker and serious journalist can put this one on his expense sheet and grab a flight to Islamabad."

The group gusted with amusement, which I ended with a cold question to Robbins. "Why can't we talk about the case as far as Robert is concerned? Why don't you report about the woman who left the Commission with Robert?"

There was a momentary silence while the group deflated from world politics to the humdrum facts of a local crime.

"Ah, yes," Robbins said, "Sir Robert left the Commission building before the meeting at the Sheraton Hotel with a Pakistani woman. His secretary says he left without telling her anything of his plans. He slipped out when she was away from her desk and she just caught sight of him leaving. He ignored a conflicting meeting with World Bank officials."

"What kind of woman?" Bradshaw asked.

"All Mrs Masood could say was that she was a Pakistani woman, who was well-dressed in the European style," Robbins replied.

Perhaps this was the girlfriend Emma suspected. An afternoon's pleasure in prospect, which actually turned out to be…

"I think we've taken this as far as we can for the moment," Leighton said. People began to rise from the padded depths of their chairs.

"How do you know the note relates to Robert if he wasn't mentioned?" I asked, and everybody halted.

Robbins looked at Hall and Hall made a head movement, clearing his junior to proceed. "Because below the main text of the note it mentions that Petrie had his testicles stuffed into the pocket of his suit. This was a fact known only to the police surgeon, senior police and Special Branch," said Robbins, with a queer smile.

9

When I returned to my apartment at 6pm, Emma was there dressed in a scanty frock. The dining table was laid for a supper for two, with a silver-plated champagne bucket, candles and flowers around the room.

"Ashraf is really very good, Nick. He's been a great help. I thought we'd have a little secret supper together later." She pirouetted in the centre of the room.

I embraced her, delighted. I wasn't too concerned about the menu. "I was expecting to see you tonight, but I didn't quite anticipate this."

"Make a couple of martinis first," she whispered.

"First? Before what?"

"Oh, I don't know. A game of cribbage," she laughed.

We each had two very dry, vodka martinis on the terrace. I told her about the meeting at the Residence. "Macbeth was there, exuding hatred of me."

"Oh, don't be silly, Nick. What did he say?"

"Nothing. We never spoke."

"How can you assume so much if you never spoke?"

"It's what I feel, that's all."

I was now sorry I had even mentioned the man. It had spoiled our shared mood of gaiety. I started to talk about Grace Stewart and described what she was wearing as though she was on the catwalk. Emma liked foolery. Our interlude finished in a warm haze and we retired to the bedroom.

Later, we sipped champagne before dinner. Ashraf

uncorked a bottle of my expensive sauvignon blanc to go with the fish. I put an Ella Fitzgerald on the Bose, very low.

"Nick, darling," Emma said, giving me a faux demure look and creating a pause so that she could be sure she had my attention. "I want you to tell me about the money." Her dark blue eyes shone.

My sensual reverie evaporated. "What money?"

"Now it's my turn to accuse you of bullshitting," she laughed.

"Savings, Emma, that's all. Savings I'm going to take to the bank."

"Darling, I prowled round this lovely room last night when you were in the bathroom. You had more money behind that Persian screen than I've ever seen. And it's all gone now, I notice. Don't tell me it was savings. You're as poor as Robert."

"All right. It was a party donation!" I gave a hearty guffaw to show I had been joking. "Just trying to impress you."

But she was seriously interested. "Really? Made to Robert?"

"Yes. I'm taking charge of it because if it was found among Robert's possessions, it would be– "

"Misunderstood."

"Exactly. You remember Robbins asked you about overseas bank accounts. So, let's keep quiet about it."

"What have you done with it?" she asked, eyes wide.

"It's better you don't know."

"It's not here?"

"You've searched the place, have you? No, it's not here."

"Do you know who it's from?"

"Yes, several companies who want to do business in Britain. It was in our private safe. Robert had mentioned it to me but I forgot about it until–"

"How do you know it's a donation?"

"Because Robert said it was and he had too much at stake to take a bribe."

The corners of her mouth turned down doubtfully. "Unless he thought he could get away with it."

"I don't believe it." I was speaking the truth because I believed Robert was honest – or, at least, I used to. I hadn't really concluded my thoughts about the contents of the 'Wilson' bag.

She caught my glance quickly. "No, you don't believe it, Nick. I believe you don't believe. It's one of the… touching things about you. How much money is it?"

"A couple of hundred thousand dollars."

"Oh, wow! Why don't we spend some of it? I'd love a Cartier watch, Nick. Buy it before Gerald does." She had a wicked twinkle in her eyes.

The man had intruded again. "Is he likely to buy you things?"

"Let's not go there, Nick. Let's have a lovely time here."

"Robert might come back at any moment. Don't forget that."

"He wouldn't know."

"That wouldn't work. Robert would see your new watch and bracelets and the smile on your face. He'd know."

So, she had a relationship with Macbeth that could entail presents of jewellery! I boiled but I didn't show it. I spoke decisively and coldly. "The only way to deal with the money is to put it on ice and see what happens to Robert. If he doesn't come back, I will get in touch with the companies who have donated and confirm that I have passed the money on. They are going to want to know."

Emma would be contemptuous of me if I took an

unduly puritanical line, but she was so taken with her own thoughts that she ignored what I said.

"If Robert doesn't come back…" she mused, "it'll be like an insurance payment." She was revelling in the idea. Then, the quality of her voice changed. "But there's a danger in it for you, Nick, just the same as there is for Robert."

"There is. It's a secret we two will have to keep." The idea of Emma keeping a secret did not seem conceivable, but I had no alternative.

Grace Stewart was installed in an office near Robert's and I spent time working with her there. She absorbed the papers I gave her very quickly and we discussed issues in a friendly way. She had a wide knowledge of the history and tribal nature of the area, which I lacked. It was clear that I was going to be in the back seat at any talks, fetching papers and carrying messages.

On the first afternoon when we had nearly finished our work, she said to me, "You don't really like any of this, do you? You're worried about Robert Laidlaw and you only came here to help him."

It was a flattering assessment of my motives. "That's about it."

"You're being a great help to me."

"You can manage without me."

"I'd like you to stick around, Nick. Something's bound to come up where I need you."

I took that as an indication that I was a useful but temporary tool. "OK. I'm not exactly over-committed at the moment."

"Fine. How do you think the investigation's going?" she asked, in a slightly patronising manner.

"Robbins isn't getting anywhere. How could he? An

assassin pops up out of 180 million souls and disappears. The cops couldn't find Robert in Chundrigar Road. We only learn what Pakistani security wants us to learn."

"You think Sir Robert's dead then?"

"I was thinking of the worst case. Let's say kidnapper instead of assassin."

She nodded, thinking. "It casts a shadow over the talks. Speculation. Mistrust."

"Bugger the talks. Let's find Robert."

"Oh, certainly. Poor man," Grace Stewart said, submerging her analytical voice in a gush of warmth. "And I know you're not serious in what you've just said about the talks."

10

At 10am the next morning, Robbins came to my office without an appointment. He appeared preoccupied; he was on a mission. His composure and neatness were unnerving. I fingered the loose knot of my own tie and decided against tightening it.

"We've had some unusual information about Sir Robert. It's about the receipt of money. It's said he received large sums…" Robbins let his words hang in the air, watching me closely.

I turned cold inside. "You mean bribes?" I raised my voice to emphasise my incredulity.

"Could be."

"That's ridiculous. Inspector, I am as close to him as anybody and I'd have known if it was true. He's a rising politician and diplomat. The game wouldn't be worth it."

Robbins continued, ignoring me. "We have information that large sums were paid to Sir Robert by companies seeking contracts. Maybe Sir Robert didn't deliver on a promise."

"But you've already established a political motive for the abduction– the Whatsit Faction."

"True, but its possible Sir Robert was turned over to the terrorists– effectively sold by those who thought they had been cheated."

I thought that it was equally possible that Macbeth, as part of his vendetta, could have passed Robert to the IF.

I was trapped with the money now. If it really was

bribe money, I was going to have to decide what to do immediately. The moment was passing when I might credibly claim the money was a political donation.

"What's the source of your information?" I asked.

"Very reliable."

"You mean not the usual thieves and addicts, but somebody in government or one of the big companies?"

"I can't discuss my informants."

"Rubbish. You're not a cop on the beat. You're not on the Pakistani force. You're an agent of the British Government."

"The same rules apply," Robbins said, heavily.

"They damn well don't! Somebody could be trying to smear Robert. That's why the source is important. If you won't reveal it, you're putting it outside my power to help."

"Why would anybody want to smear Sir Robert?"

"To discredit the British Government or, perhaps, because of enmity in private life."

"The latter seems far-fetched. Do you know anybody who might have it in for him?"

I had nursed my thoughts about Macbeth, which seemed at one moment entirely credible and at another, far-fetched. I could say something now. "Robert and Macbeth are enemies because of something that happened many years ago. It was over a woman. Macbeth was charged with rape in Britain and the charge was dropped. Robert had a part in it."

"I never knew anything about that," Robbins mused, with a small smile. "I'll bear it in mind."

"No, do more than that. Have a look at your secret informants and see if they have anything to do with Macbeth. Remember, the information is tainted."

"OK, I will," Robbins said, thoughtfully. "Now, do you know where Sir Robert might have kept any money?"

"Oh, shit! Are we still on that? No idea," I snapped.

"Surely, his safe."

"The idea's nonsense."

"About the safe, Nick. You never mentioned it. I thought you gave me a complete account of where I might find Sir Robert's papers."

"You won't find anything there except old history. Empty bottles and dirty glasses."

"You never mentioned it."

"Why should I?"

"You wouldn't have touched anything there, would you, Nick? I mean, removed anything?"

"Certainly not." I could see now that both Robert and I could be damned by the money. Events had moved too far to make it possible to argue that it was a donation.

"I suppose your prints are there, Nick?"

"I expect so. I presume you'll ask me before you start checking up on my fingerprints."

"Routine, sir."

I felt isolated. Robbins was treating me as a suspect. I watched him as if he was a scorpion, threatening and poisonous. Robbins was smart. He was an expert in Pakistani relations, one of the cream of those recruited to Special Branch and given political and language training. There was something of the military man in mufti about him: the shining black brogues, the tight uniform fit of the jacket, the club tie. Why did he choose to work in this alien environment? It wasn't because he was second-rate and couldn't succeed in Australia or Britain, that was certain. Robbins had spent a lot of his time at border posts in the Punjab or in one of the patrolling police launches in the delta of the Indus, picking up and interrogating refugees. It puzzled me why a man would prefer that to a comfortable job in Australia, with a spacious home and a more mild climate. But Robbins wasn't an ordinary man or an ordinary cop, and I was wary of him.

"You went back to your office on Wednesday night after leaving work?"

"I did. Am I being followed?" I was struggling to appear at ease.

"We keep tabs on everybody in an affair like this. Have you ever thought you might be at risk?"

"No. I'm quite… careful."

"You came out of the High Commission carrying a bag that night. What was in it?"

Robbins was watching my reactions and I wondered if the involuntary quivering of my throat was visible. The security guards had remembered. And my signature was in the log with the timing of my visit.

"Look, I went to a bar to have a drink and to read the newspaper. Then, I went back to my office to collect my towel and gym gear and get to my car."

"The bag you were carrying had sports gear in it?"

I nodded. Robbins managed his sharkish smile. "I'm sure you as a lawyer know better than most the penalty for being involved with the money we're talking about."

"Which is imaginary."

"Did you open the safe, by any chance, that evening?"

"No."

"Did you know Sir Robert's safe has an electronic record of opening and closing times?"

"No." I spoke dismissively, but I felt weak. Robbins was closing in on me.

"The safe was opened at the time you were in the office that night."

"I can't explain that." I couldn't say anything else.

"And the latest prints on the safe handle appear to be yours."

"I'd challenge that. And I'm surprised you've taken my prints without telling me."

"This is a criminal investigation."

"It's way off track."

"And, finally, Nick, only you and Sir Robert had the key."

"But I'm not keeper of Robert's key. His secretary has it. Listen, Robbins, have you forgotten that you're supposed to be finding the terrorists who have abducted Robert? Not poking about with an imaginary bribery case!"

My desperate bullying set Robbins back for a moment. "All aspects have to be considered. If Sir Robert had been taking bribes, it would be damaging for the government whether he's alive or dead."

I raised my voice. "Do your job, man, or by God I'll have you removed!"

Robbins stood up and left the room without a word or a glance, but perhaps chastened. I could see ugly reality. What a bloody fool I was, playing around with a million dollars or more of somebody else's money. It could be the end of my reputation, my easy life, my future in Britain if I was charged with obtaining the money dishonestly. Imprisonment would be vile anywhere, but in a Pakistani prison… I'd have to get rid of the money.

I immediately went along the passage to Rashida Masood's office. She was sitting straight-backed at her word processor, fingers flying to deliver a report for Grace.

"Where is Robert's key to the safe, Rashida?"

She paused. "Locked in my filing cabinet, Nick. Perfectly safe. Inspector Robbins used it. I have a note in my book. Date, time, purpose."

"Who else before that?"

A long polished fingernail traced the entry in her register. "Raj Hussein on the third of the month for filing."

"Nobody else around that time?"

"Sir Robert, himself. The morning of the day he disappeared."

Was it conceivable that before he went to lunch that day, he received the money and put it in his safe?

"Could anybody else have had access to the key?"

"No. Nobody knew it was in the cabinet except me."

I ignored this flawed reasoning and asked Rashida to call Raj. He was a polite man who looked boyish, but was actually in his fifties. He had worked at the High Commission for years. He had basic clerical skills and could write painstakingly accurate English in a beautiful script. He fetched and carried files and messages, and was regarded as utterly reliable.

Raj came into the room and stood to attention in his baggy grey denim jacket and trousers. I asked him whether the key had remained in his possession when he had used it. He looked at Rashida and they conversed in Sindhi, Rasidha saying "Uh-huh," and drumming her fingernails on the edge of the keyboard of her computer.

"OK," she said, turning to me. "He's a little upset. He was asked to give the key to the engineer who checks the safe mechanism and it was returned to him in an hour. Sounds all right to me."

When Raj had gone, I put my hand on Rashida's shoulder playfully. "Thanks," I said, conscious of the inappropriateness of the gesture. She giggled, her eyes flaring. "Just to be sure, could you check with the maintenance people?"

"Sure. You take some convincing, don't you?"

I asked Rashida about the electronic record of the safe openings. "Oh, that! There's a cabinet on the wall in the computer room. There's a dial inside but it doesn't work, hasn't for months. We have an order in with the suppliers to fix it. Inspector Robbins was having a look at it."

"I see, that's… interesting," I said. The relief I felt didn't show, but it made me feel very warm. I wasn't caught in a lie at all. Robbins had been trying to bluff an admission out of me, knowing that an electronic record of the timing of my entry would be virtually conclusive. I would have to keep in mind what a tricky character he was.

"Don't forget to ring me at home if I'm not in the office, Rashida. You've got my number."

She said nothing and didn't look at me, but quivered with pleasure. My request to be called at home was an invitation to an increased intimacy, which I felt I needed to offer to keep Rashida on my side.

11

That night I was getting out of my car, which was drawn up near the entrance to the apartments, and hauling a briefcase and a laptop off the back seat, when I heard the snarl of a moped. I looked up to see it revving down the road toward me with a helmeted driver and passenger. I quickly crossed the road to the lobby of the apartments. I was conscious that the urgent wail of the moped suddenly dropped away. The rider had closed the throttle. At the same time, a shower of bullets shattered the glass panels in the doorway. The bike sped past and then accelerated. I wasn't hit, but one of the Sikh security guards in the lobby was wounded in the shoulder.

When the ambulance had been called and the guard had received attention from a first-aider, I went upstairs, had a very large whisky and rang Robbins. He listened without comment and said, "The security on the apartments isn't enough. Tomorrow, I'll detail somebody to stay in your flat."

I accepted. My life was more important to me than my privacy. "I thought it was a half-baked attack."

"Not meant for you?"

"Meant for any infidel, perhaps."

"Maybe. We can't take that chance."

Not long after, I had a telephone call from Rashida. I was surprised at her almost instantaneous response to my invitation. She had never called me at home before. She was playfully personal when she found out I was alone. Had I eaten? What was I going to have? Why wasn't I out chasing girls? She questioned me in an amused, sensual, suggestive way. She was ringing from her home. Her husband was at his club playing snooker.

"I thought you'd like to know something odd, Nick. About Sir Robert's safe. The engineers with the maintenance contract have no record of the visit. I called them immediately after you left. They say there was no visit."

"Maybe somebody who wanted to look over the papers in the safe fooled Raj." I wasn't going to tell her the reason for my query. I was relieved to hear that there was a doubt about who had access.

"Are you going to complain about Raj?"

"No."

"Nick, he also told me something very strange. He said a man approached him saying he had a film of the Sheraton and wanted $500 for it."

"It could be a video taken from the surveillance cameras." Robbins had so far been silent about them and I hadn't pressed him. I began to wonder how reliable Raj Hussein was. "Rashida, tell him that I'll pay the money."

Rashida was surprised, but that was a conversation she was putting off until tomorrow. She wanted to get personal. "It's so nice talking to you like this, Nick. You make me feel good."

I was slightly shocked by the attack that evening and huddling in the warmth of Rashida's voice wasn't unpleasant.

"Tell me what you're doing," I said, feebly.

"I'm not wearing very much, just a silk slip."

"Nothing else?"

"Nothing," she said, softly. "I'm on the bed. I could pull the slip up…"

We didn't get to telephone sex, but I suspected we could have. After a few more moments, I lied that there was somebody at the door. My head ached.

I dined alone. It was one of Ashraf's more or less palatable attempts at chicken curry, but the sauce had a fishy tang like no other chicken I'd ever tasted. I left most of the meal and began to walk around the apartment. The rooms had an emptiness without Emma. All signs of her presence had been eliminated by Ashraf's meticulous daily cleaning.

I tried to watch TV but was quickly bored. What was in this film that Raj could buy? I couldn't concentrate on a book. The pile of working papers I had in my briefcase were not compelling. I had a few more shots of Scotch and listened to a classical CD. By the time I went into the bedroom, it was late– nearly 12am– and I was slightly drunk.

I took off my casual clothes, dropping them on the floor for Ashraf to pick up in the morning. I didn't switch the lights on, but looked out on the jewelled glow of Islamabad and Rawalpindi. I then slipped into the bathroom, showered and threw myself on top of the white counterpane on the bed, naked and damp. The air conditioning was switched off and it was quiet.

I had been unable to find out from Emma whether she was seeing Macbeth regularly. She enjoyed taunting me with the possibility that she was. She couldn't see that in trying to create some kind of relationship with Macbeth, she was playing with a live grenade. Gerald Macbeth was a person I had hoped at one time to never see again or to be anywhere near. To be in a country where he was a powerful force was a dangerous situation.

I wasn't sure that Macbeth would direct his ire at me

personally. I was only a minor irritant and so I discounted the idea that he could have had anything to do with the attack tonight. He certainly had the untraceable power to have ordered it, but if he wanted to kill me he could surely find more sure and effective means.

Macbeth and Robert had been friends at one time. They had spent their summers in the same colonial society, moving between exclusive clubs for swimming and tennis, and flying backwards and forwards to school in England on the same aircraft. When I met them, the rivalry had already developed. They no longer spoke to each other and I never found out what the precise cause of their falling-out had been. Perhaps there was no single event, but rather a vague, childish jealousy that had been compounded by imagined insults on either side.

At first, Macbeth had impressed me. He was what I aspired to be and once thought I was: the scholar-athlete beloved of the English public schools. He had been marked as a future head of house and possibly head of school. The masters thought Macbeth was mature because they saw him as a parcel of singular achievements– a fast miler, a useful winger on the rugby field, a top oarsman, a fine student who was as good at languages as he was at maths.

The boys were more pragmatic, though, and Macbeth was mildly disliked by many. He behaved in a superior manner. His most frequent form of address was scornful and derisory. He was also a manipulative person who wielded influence over a band of carefully nurtured cronies.

Robert, when I met him, was quite different. He couldn't quite surpass Macbeth's scholarship or sporting achievements, though he was a threatening competitor in both. He had charisma. I felt it in our first meeting in the smelly March House cloakroom. When he said something was so, others were inclined to believe him. He could be good-natured and protective; he made his friends feel that they were important to him. He was absolutely never boring. I used to think of him as the Pied Piper (although I was uncertain where he was leading us), or as a Greek god must be– not merely beautiful, but irresistible.

When I entered March House, Robert and Macbeth were in their sixth form year and there was an undeclared struggle for the headship of the house in the next year. Macbeth was the official favourite. While the senior boys were consulted about the appointment, success depended on convincing the housemaster, Larsen, who was a former rugby international with a gammy knee. Larsen was feeling the strain of his job. He was under forty and his hair had turned snow white. The current head of house, a maths wizard who went on to distinguish himself at Harwell, had no capacity for leadership. He was a boffin. March House tottered dysfunctionally behind the other houses, and the authority to make it work smoothly came from uneasy truces between those who supported Laidlaw and the followers of Macbeth.

This was the effect of the rift between the pair. Each had set himself up as a kind of baron with his own fiefdom. In hindsight it was ridiculous and trivial, but at the time it was what conditioned our lives.

12

I was at the office early and accompanied the British team to a conference room at the Marriott hotel near the diplomatic enclave, for talks with an Afghan Government delegation. We walked along Constitution Avenue past the Presidency and the National Assembly, which sat comfortably in well-watered lawns and suggested a majestic solidity that must have been the object of its European architect.

I was with the party as they waited for proceedings to begin, but was not invited to the talks. My main value was my knowledge of Robert's papers and the line he had taken at other meetings. I had had a dialogue with Grace up to this moment, but she wanted to stamp her leadership on the delegation and I suppose didn't want to be publicly reliant on me.

She looked self-possessed in one of her neat linen suits. Bradshaw was there, joking as usual, as well as a Pakistani woman secretary and two other young male assistants from the Foreign Office team. One of them, David Griffiths, a Welshman who was usually quietly drunk by late afternoon, I had found to be quite convivial company.

We were in that peculiar hiatus that I knew well as a practising barrister: the period that immediately precedes an important meeting or a court hearing, in which people are too preoccupied to socialise except in a perfunctory way, and yet have completed all their preparations and have nothing to do. Grace and her team circled each other, muttering banalities.

This was to be a meeting about a meeting to be held later in Kabul. It would decide 'the shape of the table': who would attend, the subjects to be discussed, and the wording and order of the agenda. Grace had a long list of items to cover which was tucked in her briefcase. The talks, although they would appear to be about incidental subjects, would give each side a good idea where the other stood without openly saying a word about the issues. I had a foreboding, though— not so much of failure, but of the futility of the mission. It would be a small party of mostly white bureaucrats trying to settle the turbulent affairs of a tribal nation far away to the north. It seemed arrogant and the Afghans recognised this. I made sure that Grace had everything she wanted, wished her good luck and departed.

Just before lunch, when I was thinking of going to the Pakistan Club for a drink, Bradshaw put his head around the door of my office.

"All over?" I asked.

"We came back with our tails down," he said, scarcely able to conceal his amusement at Grace's discomfort. "They don't really want to talk to the second team."

"So, no progress?"

"No progress, but plenty of excuses to have another meeting in Kabul."

"Sort of diplomatic tourism."

"That's what the job's really about. Let's go over to the club."

When I arrived back at my office, Rashida Masood handed me the film that Raj Hussein had obtained with the money I had given him from Robert's hoard. Rashida was expecting a compliment from me, but I was too engrossed to carry our flirtation another step forward. I rang Robbins and told him of my discovery. When I said I wasn't sure if the High Commission had the right equipment to project the film, he suggested I come to his office.

When I arrived, Robbins had a digital projector on the desk. He quickly fixed a screen on the wall and pulled the slatted blinds closed. "We should get a bigger, clearer picture if we see it on a screen, rather than on a monitor," he said.

In a few seconds, the machine was running. I felt excited and sickened. We were going to be taken to the scene of a murder.

I saw a blurred, bluish corridor in a building. Nothing appeared to move for a time.

"It's the Sheraton," Robbins said.

Then, two Pakistani girls holding hands came down the hall toward us. There was a pause. A man and a woman came into view. The man was definitely Robert, hands in his pockets and a hank of hair hanging over his forehead. He was swaying jauntily as he approached the door of the fateful room. The woman with him was a tall Pakistani in a black costume and a white blouse, aged in her thirties. She had her shining black hair piled on top of her head and pendant earrings. Her high cheekbones and eyes were heavily made up – she was just the sort of woman Robert would have found alluring in a casual way. Robert, entry card in hand, opened the door of 1062 and the pair went inside.

A few seconds later, a small, grey-bearded Pakistani of around sixty, with a bald head and a shiny grey suit, came down the corridor. He stopped at 1062, knocked and was admitted.

"Petrie's not there," I said, as the film came to an end. "And how did Robert and the woman get out, and Petrie get in?"

"It's what I'd like to know. This is the only extant film

from the surveillance videos. I've had a look at everything that they have at the hotel."

"It looks suspicious, doesn't it, Inspector? A crucial event in the corridor not recorded."

"It does, unless it's plain incompetence. The management say they've been having trouble with the camera mechanism on and off and haven't been able to get anybody to service it."

"That sounds very convenient. You haven't reported any of this at the meeting."

"I'm conducting the investigation, not you, Nick. I can't report every detail at the meeting."

"What do you make of it?" I asked.

"I can't make anything at the moment."

"Well, I can. If somebody interfered with the cameras, it implies a more sophisticated hand than terrorists usually have. Remember what I said about Macbeth?"

Robbins was impassive. "Maybe."

"The woman is startlingly noticeable if she's local. Surely somebody could identify her?"

"I'll look into it."

"Do more than that, Inspector. Rashida Masood says Robert left the High Commision building with a woman. If she was shown a photo, she might be able to recognise the woman."

"As I said, I'll look into it."

"And the man?"

"We'll try photo recognition on the computer database. It's fairly accurate."

"We can nail the woman, surely."

"Can we get a line on the people who handed the film to you?"

"I doubt it. I tried to get Hussein to identify the man

who made the offer to him and delivered the film, but he said it was a messenger."

"There's hundreds, probably thousands, of them," Robbins said.

On Saturday morning I had lunch with Grace Stewart at the Malaysian Club– a yellow-green, coconut-flavoured curry. I cooled my mouth with iced beer. The date of the Kabul meeting had been settled and it was approaching fast, with many minor issues unsettled. The Afghans were effectively refusing to deal with anybody but Robert. They were irritated with us for, as it were, losing Robert. It may have been that they had special understandings with him about the deployment of aid and contracts for reinstatement.

Grace didn't know Robert Laidlaw. For her, he didn't exist except as a problem. She was preoccupied with whether she could conduct the talks successfully. If she could, her career would advance. If the talks produced little or nothing, she was unlikely to be blamed, but might be regarded as somebody who could have done better.

"You don't want Robert to be found, do you, Grace?"

"I wouldn't put it that way, Nick. If he hadn't been abducted, I wouldn't be here. I was lucky to be appointed, but I already had a good job and this might be a poisoned chalice. We have a lot of trouble on our hands as a result. If he's not found it'll be a tragedy, but we'll get on and do the job. If he is found, there'll be an international fuss. Then there are these awful allegations of bribery, which will surface publicly at some stage."

"So, on balance, it's better he's not found."

"I didn't say that, Nick."

"Look, Grace, I have a difficulty with Robbins. He's not getting anywhere."

"Yes, I've heard your remarks at the meetings."

"Do you give him instructions, Grace?"

"No, of course not. As you know, he's under the High Commissioner– through Leonard Hall– and he works with the Pakistani police."

"Grace, does he have access to your Top Secret files?"

"No, certainly not. In the remote likelihood that he needs to know anything, he'll be told."

"But how does he learn what he needs to know without the opportunity to search the files?"

Grace smiled. "Nick, those files are about political issues miles away from abduction and murder."

"No, Grace, they're also about people. And people commit murder and abduction."

"If there was something he wanted, he could ask Leonard Hall. Leonard has access as a senior intelligence officer to everything except a small category of political files."

"So even Leonard Hall doesn't get to see the full picture!"

I stared at this prim, confident woman, who met my eyes so frankly and rested her unadorned, elegant white hands on the table in a relaxed way. My scepticism of the intelligence maze was showing.

I showered when I reached my apartment, changed my suit for a T-shirt and light slacks, and sat on the open terrace looking over the lawns below. I was listlessly re-reading *Pride and Prejudice* to make a little cultural progress.

The man assigned by Robbins to guard me was a Karachi-born Indian named Vincent Ram, who took up residence in one of the two spare bedrooms. He was a junior Special Branch inspector, very quiet and discreet, with thick steel hair and rimless glasses that seemed to magnify his eyeballs. I felt better having him in the apartment, although it was inhibiting. He was interesting on Islamabad life and he played a mean game of poker.

The fact that Ram would routinely search the place made me feel secure, but under surveillance. No doubt Special Branch were still looking for the money or a clue to where the money might be. The apartment was a less homely place now. I had initially enjoyed the rooms and had created a private space for myself, but that was gone.

It was the usual humid late afternoon, but a hazy sun had been replaced by silver clouds and sudden rushes of hot air. I tried to work out what the next move should be to find Robert. Although Robbins kept talking about keeping up the pace of the investigation, I wasn't convinced that he was moving as fast as he could or should. It may have been because of the man's deliberate ways. I had occasionally been told that something was to be done 'Islamabad style', which meant moving without deliberate haste. Perhaps Robbins was proceeding in the way in which this community had educated him.

He was the one person amongst the British contingent who was in touch with the police and the street. He wasn't alone in speaking Urdu and Sindhi fluently, but he was the only one who could translate the strange ways of the underworld of Islamabad and Rawalpindi into meaningful terms. Without him, the so-called committee would be forced to put their feet up and forget about Robert.

The other probability about Robbins was that he was more than a sleuth trying to catch a criminal. He was a specialist in political intelligence. He was used to venturing in poisoned waters, where allegiances are not straightforward. Solving the crime could be one goal of his, but I thought a more important objective was to do a job that pleased his masters– the High Commissioner and the Foreign Office.

On the surface, we were all were striving for the same objective: to find Robert as soon as possible, albeit with a disgracefully undermanned investigatory force. However, there was a point where interests diverged. Another objective was to avoid international embarrassment; another to protect diplomatic relations with Afghanistan and Pakistan. A further vital concern, placing incalculable stress on the investigation, was the personal interests of the seekers for preferment: Grace Stewart, Hugh Leighton and Geoffrey Bradshaw. I therefore had a vague suspicion, no more than that, when I considered how effective Robbins' activities might be.

I began to think of what I might do myself. This wasn't the place where a Sherlock Holmes or a Philip Marlowe could step in and conjure a solution. We Europeans were on the outside. Even Robbins could only work through his network of loyal local police and informers. I went to bed with the depressing sense that the search for Robert had stalled.

13

At the High Commissioner's Residence meeting on Monday, I interrupted the airy exchanges and suggested that two or three more inspectors of the same calibre as Robbins should be appointed and should work to a reviewable plan. I said I wasn't casting aspersions at Robbins; it was more a question of manpower. I explained very delicately that as Robert was a distinguished politician, the efforts of one lone Special Branch inspector, in what was a grave case involving murder, was inadequate.

Robbins jolted back in his chair as though I had punched him in the chest, but said nothing. The others were startled and looked at Hall. Hall took offence.

"Is Mr Dyson criticising my competence?" he asked with a chesty harrumph of disapproval. "Mr Robbins has the full support of all the Commission's resources, and the local police."

I tried to explain that we were not actually investigating Robert's disappearance in the sense of moving forward and achieving objectives, but were adrift, rudderless. "A note is handed in at a police station. An informer gives some information. We find a film showing Robert. Our knowledge enlarges a little, but the initiative always remains with the terrorists. We appear to be a mere listening post."

This view was received very quietly by the group. Their chill and the lack of any reply indicated the gravity of my faux pas. Even Bradshaw, who could be relied on for a quip on the most grisly occasion, was silent.

The group looked to Leighton, who seemed to be measuring his own vulnerability. He spoke after a moment. "I'm perfectly satisfied with the progress of the enquiry, Nick. Leonard, I think you're managing it in the customary way."

He ended with a gentle finality that quashed me. The others murmured approval. Afterwards, I slunk away from the meeting on my own.

When I analysed my feelings, I was ambivalent about Robert. He was a kind of friend, he had an attractive personality and he promised advancement for me. The other side was, admittedly, jealousy about Emma. Right now, though, I was angered by the tardiness of the investigation. Robert wasn't going to be short-changed over police support if I could help it.

I thought of the money in its hiding place (a locked trunk, left with one of my neighbours in the block of flats). I would, if I had to, justify what I was doing as protecting Robert. If I was found with the money, I would have no alternative but to say it was a party donation on its way back to London, and that it had been given to me by Robert for safekeeping. I would explain that I had placed it with a neighbour because there were concerns over my own safety and the security of my apartment (as I had told my neighbour without disclosing the true contents). Was that really credible, though? I didn't know who the donor was and an honest man, questioned as I had been by Robbins, would at least have mentioned it. It wasn't exactly a forgettable item when there was an issue about receipt of corrupt payments. I had a gnawing worry.

That evening I took Emma to the Sky Room Restaurant at the Hilton, not troubled if we were seen together. Emma, herself, didn't care; she was anything but the grieving wife. She seemed to love and hate Robert, and returned his unfaithfulness in the same coin. She made herself free for me, and we were going to enjoy ourselves with the best food and service in Islamabad. I had kept a stash of dollars from Robert's pile to cover eventualities like this.

Originally, my idea in asking Emma to dinner was to get her to think about returning to England with me. Good food and wine would make it possible to discuss such a delicate subject. Part of me had given up hope that Robert would ever be found alive. I didn't know whether Emma shared that view. My own career in Islamabad, such as it had been, was finished if Robert didn't return. I wasn't popular with the Foreign Office because I wasn't one of them. They wouldn't take kindly to giving succour to one of Robert's imports.

I couldn't leave the country without resolving my relations with Emma. Now, as I sipped a double gin and tonic, I was elated by the liquor. I looked over the gleaming table cloths of the Sky Room under discreet lamps, laden with silver and crystal. The idea of bolting with Emma seemed emotional and extravagant. Even the jazzed up Vivaldi in the background couldn't sanitise the thought.

While the likelihood that Robert would return was becoming more remote with every day that passed, I was also troubled by the need to stay until there was some resolution. I owed Robert that much. I tried to explain these thoughts to Emma, but by the time I had drunk two G&Ts and half a bottle of red wine and had finished the specially imported New York steak, I was stumbling incoherently. To my surprise– I never knew how Emma was going to react– she rounded on me in irritation, not in the least impressed that I wanted to take care of her after the resolution of the Robert question.

"You speak as though Robert was dead! And we don't know that yet! He could walk through the door at any moment!" she said.

"And you'd want to stay with him, Emma?"

"And you'd want to work for him!"

Emma was only eighteen when I had first seen her, then an assistant matron at March House, Poole Abbey. Her fragile, fine-boned face, the frame of brown curls and the litheness of her body beneath the flimsy smock she wore on duty inflamed my senses. Like most of the boys, I was very susceptible. At that time, I carried her image in the forefront of my mind like the icon of a saint.

I used to spend my holidays in isolation from other children, usually with my aunt at her cottage in Salisbury. To me, Aunt Lily seemed asexual. Very rarely, I spent some part of the vacation with my father, who would be making a business trip to an exotic place. I could be looking at the Roman ruins at El Djem while other kids were lying on a beach in Devon with their girlfriends. I hardly knew anything about girls then. I remembered the daughter of the headmaster of the Grange Preparatory School in Fordingbridge, who, with her hair cut short and wearing short pants, had attended the otherwise all-boy classes. As head boy, it was acceptable for me to walk with Melanie in the extensive grounds, well out of sight of others. We discovered each other in the bushes without any clear understanding of what might be done after the first fumbling revelations. Later, I had feelings for Dorothy Martin, the matron at March House. She found me on the day I arrived, sitting on my trunk in the cloakroom, smarting at the loss of my tennis racket. She had my trunk transported to the six-bed dormitory on the first floor. The blankets on the beds were bright blue, the walls white, and the floor was made up of highly polished golden boards. She was part mother, part girlfriend to all of us, this former army nurse of thirty-five. Dorothy seemed to me neither a girl or a woman. Her voluptuous body radiated warmth and the luck of brushing her breast or thigh kept dreams alive for days. My feelings for Dorothy were similar to those I had for Melanie; they were carnal. I used to imagine Dorothy's naked body descending upon me, smothering me.

Emma Southern was far from this incarnation. I had no fleshy thoughts about Emma at that time. My love for her was pure and ethereal. She made me ache inside. I wanted to show her I was a hero. Everything I did that required nerve was done for her. She was an unattainable star. Now, I laughed out loud about this. All our relationship had amounted to then, was her questioning my spurious need for so many aspirins. It was not until the night I heard the scream that I focused on her as a sexual being– and perhaps not precisely then, but a day or so later.

14

I was sat under an umbrella on the lawn at the High Commissioner's residence, listening to Grace Stewart dwelling on the lack of cooperation from the Afghans in resuming talks. "They've seized on Sir Robert's disappearance and the fuss it's generated as a pretext for backing off."

A garden sprinkler made a pleasing thrum as it watered the lush garden. "My impression is that they want to deal with Robert," I said.

"Lovely as Robert is," said Bradshaw, who was sitting with us, "I don't think it's entirely that. It's money, or the solemn promise of it, that brings them to the table. Unless we have that, we have nothing. They're not interested in our fussy, nit-picking kind of diplomacy."

"We have money and we have contracts for reinstatement," Grace said.

"Subject to a hundred pettifogging conditions," Bradshaw replied. "Robert doesn't worry about small print."

Grace frowned. "I don't know what you mean by that. He has to follow his instructions."

"Not a man for following instructions is Robert," Bradshaw said.

"We're only here to help and to help generously…" Grace said.

"And, oh dear, our generosity evokes contempt. The

Afghans are sick of us sticking our oar into their affairs. They know their history. The message is to sod off," Bradshaw said.

Insects hummed in the soft air as I shaded my eyes against the horizon. I felt I was in a parallel universe, quite comfortable, where we played war and diplomatic games like computer games.

"You're very critical, Geoffrey," Leighton muttered, having arrived on the lawn and slumped into a deckchair in time to hear Bradshaw's last declamation.

"We still have a security role," Grace said, plaintively.

"You mean before it becomes absolutely clear to the world that our intervention has made life worse?" Bradshaw said.

"Could we speak about Robert?" I asked.

"There's been some progress," Robbins said. "I've had a message from the Independence Faction. A boy handed in the note at a police station."

"What do they want— apart from money, release of their friends from custody and the immediate retirement of the British and Americans from Afghanistan and Pakistan?" Bradshaw asked.

"They want to talk."

"Sounds like money," Bradshaw said.

"Do you know anything more about them?" I asked Robbins.

"I'm hoping to track some of their people down."

"Hoping?" I said.

"It's not easy. They are one of a dozen cliques making threats, implicated in hostage-taking and bombing. They want westerners out."

"Except as tourists and aid donors," Bradshaw said.

"Of course you'll have to talk, Dennis," Leighton said.

"I'll tell London that we're in touch with the terrorists. That, at least, is progress."

"Progress?" I said, "We have a note asking for talks. We propose to agree. This is progress? What about Robert?"

Leighton raised his eyebrows at my impudence, but narky words could not disturb the somnolent morning.

"They say they'll kill him if we try to trap them," Robbins said.

I felt energised. A sudden pulse of the heart. Robert was alive and out there somewhere! I tried to imagine where he was being held and the conditions, but here, on the lawn, sipping orange juice through a straw, I couldn't. Robbins had retained this piece of information and the others didn't seem interested. Leighton had lost patience with the meeting. He now followed everybody's comments with a clipped 'Right!' to cut them off.

"I think we ought to have a more precise idea about what we're going to do," I said, trying to make the request sound less like a complaint.

"Right!" snapped Leighton again, easing himself up.

"I think we have adequate plans in place," Hall said, tiredly.

"Right!" Leighton said, once more.

I didn't think there was any plan, let alone plural plans, but Leighton nodded emphatically in support.

"I have a suggestion," Robbins said. "Why doesn't Nick accompany me to the meeting with the IF. We'll be asking for proof that the terrorists have Sir Robert and that he's alive. Nick is one of the people who might be able to identify personal effects or other evidence on this point."

I hadn't anticipated such front-line exposure. Robbins showed the faintest flutter of amusement. The rest of the party were looking at me, enjoying my awkwardness.

Hall's tightly pursed, bloodless lips implied that I had got my just deserts for whining about the effectiveness of the investigation. It was true that if I went with Robbins I might learn something that would enable me to drive the case along more swiftly. In any event, under those several pairs of critical eyes, it was a matter of pride not to refuse.

"OK, Robbins."

"I'm afraid we won't have much back-up. We could get into trouble ourselves if they discover we're tracking them," Robbins said, looking at me and willing me to change my mind.

I was apprehensive but I tried to suppress any signs. "I don't see why they want a meeting. There's nothing they can't say in a message. How do we know it's not a set- up?"

"It's unlikely," Hall said. "Ordinary criminal kidnappers would never expose themselves. The IF don't see themselves as criminals. They think they're patriots. They want recognition as a political force. So, up to a point, they are prepared to show and identify themselves. If they wanted to kill, they could do it on the street any time."

"We may be lucky and get a lead on the IF as a result of this rendezvous," Robbins said. "We'll have somebody there to try to track them, but we'll have to go easy. We don't want to threaten Sir Robert's life."

"How many of us will there be?"

"Two," Robbins said, noticing my discomfort. "If you want me to deal with it, fine."

"I said I'd come and I will," I said, brusquely.

Robbins glanced complacently around the rest of the party, who were now standing and preparing to move.

Bradshaw laughed. "Don't agree too big a ransom and don't give away any of our colonies."

15

I had learned that the invitation to a boat party on a Sunday was as much a part of the social round as the curry lunches at the High Commissioner's Residence on Saturdays. It was a long haul to get to suitable water, but this didn't deter anybody. The invitation on this occasion came from Bradshaw, who, as a bachelor with private means, lived in style. I had come to enjoy these lazy affairs.

We had to take an interminable drive in our cars (I went with Bradshaw in his BMW) through many poor villages and small towns to assemble at Srinigat Pier on Rawal Lake in the Margalla National Park. A launch was waiting to take us out to the Princess's mooring. The yacht was a white plastic cruiser that looked like a wedding cake. We were a party of about fifteen; the men in bright sports shirts and shorts, and the women in cotton dresses with bare shoulders and legs and wide sun hats. The lake was hazed in blue. The cold water had a dark warmth and threw out arrows of red and green. I couldn't think that it was entirely clean. Snow-flecked mountains rose like a backdrop in a theatre. The main deck was shaded by a colourful awning and festive ribbons fluttered from the masts.

The guests spread themselves among the tables on the deck and Bradshaw lumbered between us serving drinks, his white shirt taut across his paunch. This task might have been done by one of the crew, but it was meant by him as a convivial joke. The clumsiness with which he fumbled glasses and bottles and mixed up orders was intended to be funny. He was hopeless at such things and proud of it.

I saw Grace Stewart off-duty for the first time; wearing a backless sundress she looked young and not very serious. Emma was a presence, carefully tanned, dressed in a flame-coloured shirt and tight white trousers to just below the knee. Her natural inclination to forget everything except the enjoyable present must have puzzled the others. Robbins brought along a handsome but inarticulate Chinese girl whom he introduced as his wife, who he had married during a tour of duty in Hong Kong.

I considered the rest of my companions: mostly British men with British wives, all between about thirty and forty, but looking older than their years. A few may have had short-term contracts, but most were expatriates– tied to Pakistan because it provided a standard of living they could not duplicate elsewhere. I had begun to experience the mentality myself; they were uncomfortable with the circumscribed life, yet were averse to the risk of going elsewhere. Many of the women were physically attractive, but they had a wary look. Pakistan was not a comfortable place for married female expatriates. Women were cloistered by the culture and there were too many cheap whores– although there was, perhaps, an ironic security in that.

The crew cruised the boat for more than an hour in the cool blue centre of the lake while we drank and chattered. At lunchtime we anchored in a deserted, bush-covered cove. The lunch was a delicious hamper of cold prawns, lobster and salad, served with rice and garlic bread.

I talked idly to everybody within range, always unwilling to stray far from Emma. We were both a little high on the gin and tonics and were enjoying each other's company.

We didn't notice a large speedboat nose into sight and drift toward us. One of our crew called out and waved.

"It's Macbeth's torpedo boat!" Bradshaw shouted, picking up a megaphone, "Ahoy, Challenger. Come and join us!"

I thought the rakish red boat with its prominent chrome exhausts looked phallic and threatening. In a moment, the day became oppressive for me.

The two vessels were quickly moored together. The three or four passengers or crew on the speedboat joined our party. There was no need for introductions; everybody appeared to know each other already. The crew served more drinks and appetisers. I hung back from the knot of talkers. Emma went up to Macbeth, resplendent in his skipper's white, peaked hat, and he kissed her cheeks. His glance fell on me and passed over me as though I wasn't there.

Later, Macbeth invited the party to ski from the back of his boat. My intimacy with Emma had been shattered and I sat miserably under the awning with Robbins and his wife, sipping beer, while many of the party took turns to ride in the speedboat and ski. Robbins leaned close to me. "Nick, there was something revolting on the internet this morning," he said, without expression.

"Petrie?"

"Yes. It showed the beheading. It looked like Petrie was on his knees in front of the bed. There was a masked executioner with a machete. He delivered the usual harangue. Then, it showed what I saw when I entered room 1062– Petrie's headless corpse sitting up against the bedhead with the banner above him on the wall."

"Horrific, but we were expecting it." I pushed my beer away. The heaviness of the day seemed to increase. I could smell the slaughterhouse. Robbins was conversing lightly with his wife. If I rebuked him for being crass, he would only reply that I always wanted to know everything at the earliest moment.

I half-watched the skiing party for a while, sometimes seeing Petrie on his knees on the carpet, sometimes Emma in the speedboat, always close to Macbeth. Everything started with Macbeth. One of the crew on the speedboat produced a mass of red silk– a parachute for parascending. Some of the men began to try it, rising high, perhaps 60 feet above the lake, with the powerful pull of the speedboat. They then cut loose and paraglided down to the lake.

Somebody on the speedboat shouted that Emma (who had already water-skiied) was going to try it. She had changed into a white bikini for the skiing and took her place at the stern of the Princess, where there was a launching step for the skiers.

Macbeth, anonymous in his commander role, skirled his boat around in a sheet of spray and sped out to the length of the tow. I could hear the muffled snarl of the boat's engine winding up. Emma took off smoothly, trailing the silk, which began to billow as her speed increased. She was soon able to slip out of her skis and rise from the surface of the lake under the bright parachute. When she had attained full height, there was a pistol shot. The tow rope had parted prematurely. Emma swung like a pendulum. The chute spilled air instead of floating free, then it crumpled. Emma plunged down, trailing the chute like a flame.

I shouted, though it was a meaningless shriek. I stood up to get a better view of the patch of red silk on the water, which was swiftly approached by the speedboat. The crew hauled up the silk and, with it, Emma's body. I couldn't see if she was conscious at that distance.

I covered my face with my hands, wanting to cry in

agony. Then I looked at the crowd on the launch platform. There, amazingly, was Emma, her white bikini and tan unmistakable. She turned to me and waved.

"I thought it was Lady Laidlaw in the water," Robbins gasped.

The speedboat came alongside us. The other woman in the white bikini was shocked and semi-conscious. Macbeth prepared the Challenger to return to the jetty with the injured woman. The fall put a damper on the whole party. Emma was very subdued.

"God, I was standing right beside her in the queue," she said.

Even Bradshaw's bonhomie could not revive us. We soon returned to shore.

16

We were to meet in the foyer of the Regent Hotel in Balucastan Place at 10am. Robbins had warned me not to be late, implying I was a burden and had to keep up. He was going to supply transport to Rawalpindi. He wanted to get into position early; his undercover people would be there well in advance to suss out the area.

I went to the lavatory at the office before setting out for the hotel. In the mirror, I could see that my debonair spirit had faded. My loose collar hung down feebly and I buttoned it. I tightened my tie for once. My usually healthy complexion had a floury pallor. I splashed cold water on my face. I confessed to the empty room that I was scared.

The minutes seemed to flick by very quickly on my wristwatch. I paced around my office thinking I was a fool for having agreed to go so far. I left the Commission. I had enough time and I walked slowly through the gardens to the hotel. Robbins was waiting at the entrance in grey slacks and a short-sleeved, white shirt. A uniformed police driver drove us in a Land Rover to the outskirts of Rawalpindi. We had a ten-minute walk before us. The Kalufi district to which we had been directed was a law unto itself, a poverty-stricken place where criminals lived like flies. Within this enclave was the café chosen for the meeting.

"We're being followed by two different teams working independently," Robbins said. "We're not going to try any tricks with the Faction. Our people will try to observe them and follow unobtrusively. If we can pick up some intelligence on where they are based, we'll work on that. Surveillance."

The Land Rover dropped us in a side street. Robbins said, "Leave your jacket in the car. Take off your tie and roll up your sleeves. We have to look clean of mikes and weapons or they won't approach us. We'll soon be under observation."

Robbins reached over and took a copy of *The Financial Times*, distinctively pink, from the back seat. "I have to carry this. It's like Berlin in the Cold War, isn't it?"

"It's a hot war and a stupid one," I replied. I didn't feel like conversing.

"And by the way, Nick. Leave the talking to me."

I picked my way down the crowded path slightly behind Robbins, who was rapping the rolled newspaper against his palm. The pair of us were about a foot taller than anybody in the street and quite conspicuous.

The scene could have been any time in the last hundred years, except for tinny noises from transistor radios hanging in the shed-like shops, the occasional miniature TV set perched on a box or a bag of rice, and the ubiquitous mobile phones clasped in brown fists. The open shop fronts displayed their specialty: dried fish, herbs, spices, fruit, pots and pans. Old men and women with yokes over their shoulders fetched and carried on the run. Boys sweated to move heavy burdens in decrepit carts. Rickshaw men shouted and pedicab drivers rang their bells incessantly in the press of traffic. The stink was sickening.

At a corner, we came to an open area of chairs and tables. Men in soiled white jackets were serving tea. An old grey tarpaulin had been strung up on bamboo poles to shade the tables.

"This is it," Robbins said. "Take a seat and we'll wait."

My initial feeling of apprehension had been overcome a little by the crowd, the noise, the confusion and the heat. "Odd place to choose."

"No, it's a good place for them," Robbins said.

We took seats where we could view the rest of the tables. Robbins placed the newspaper before him. I turned round to see a footpath streaming with people and the decrepit café building with its dark interior.

"We're really exposed here," Robbins said. "We can't protect our backs. We can be seen from every angle. A sniper's dream. When they go, they can disappear in any direction into the crowd and be untraceable in seconds."

Robbins knew he was alarming me. He was amused. I was tense and sweating copiously. Why assume that murderers were going to respect the arrangement we had with them? We ordered tea. The weak, scented liquid burned my tongue. Five minutes passed, ten and then fifteen. I began to be lulled into a lethargy that would end in a shock every minute or so, when one of the patrons or a waiter jolted my chair. Then, a woman came from behind, pushing rudely past, brushing my shoulder and stopped to look at me. She was a stocky, grey-headed Pakistani woman of perhaps sixty, in a black suit and headscarf. I felt the sweat rush out of my pores as I looked up into a pocked face wearing heavy, horn-rimmed spectacles. She drew a copy of the English language *Rawalpindi Albion* from her bag and dropped it beside *The Financial Times*.

"We'll take your chairs," the woman said in confident, American-accented English. "Get up."

She calmly sat down in my chair while Robbins and I moved around the other side of the table. A middle-aged Pakistani man with cropped, silver hair and a neat business suit, collar and tie, slid into the seat next to her. I suppose I had been expecting two men with beards in black gymsuits.

"What's this for?" I asked Robbins as we found new seats.

"Avoiding directional mikes or cameras aimed at them."

Robbins greeted the pair in Urdu. The intonations of the language seemed absurd coming from his mouth, as though he was playing games.

The woman watched him critically. When he finished, she sneered, "We'll speak in English. Listen to me carefully: we have Robert Laidlaw…"

"You killed Petrie," Robbins said.

"We executed him. And we'll execute Laidlaw if we have to. What we require is the release of Rafik Ali and Tarik Mussafa."

Robbins thought for a moment. "They're held by the Pakistani Government. Don't you understand that neither the Pakistani Government or ours will release prisoners as a ransom?" Robbins said.

"You'd rather we cut off Laidlaw's head?" the woman asked, quietly.

"I don't think we have any influence over the fate of Ali and Mussafa," Robbins said.

"Then we should kill Laidlaw now?" Her voice was low and even. She might have been referring to dropping a sheet of paper in the bin.

"No. Don't harm Robert Laidlaw," I said. "We're here to receive your message and take it back to the Foreign Office. We'll investigate the possibility of the release of the two men. We'll get in touch with you."

The woman looked at Robbins, noting with faint amusement his frown of disagreement. "Good. We'll let you know where and when the exchange can be made. Remember, the life of an important man depends upon it," she said, sarcastically.

"Can you prove Robert Laidlaw is alive?" I asked.

The man produced a small hide-covered silver flask. I took the flask, turning it over in my palm, trying to visualise the adventures it had been through, the pain it had witnessed. A plate on the side had the engraved initials RSJL. I had drunk from the flask in better days.

"You don't have anything else?" Robbins asked.

"You'll just have to have faith," the woman laughed mirthlessly.

After a pause, she removed a compact disc from her bag and slid it across the table.

"What does it show?" I asked, although I knew it must be some proof. The mere fact that she could produce it was a huge relief.

"No prizes for guessing," she said, baring her bright teeth.

"OK," Robbins said, taking the flask and the disk and pushing them into his trouser pocket. "We'll get back to you as soon as possible. How do we communicate with you?"

"We'll let you know."

"What is Laidlaw's state of health?" I asked.

The woman looked at me pitifully. "What do you expect me to say? Vermin survive in the worst possible conditions."

"That's not good enough," I said.

The woman looked round cautiously, ignoring me. "We're going now. You're being watched. You give us five minutes before leaving here. Five minutes. If you want Laidlaw back, don't blow it."

The pair rose quietly and slipped through the tables in different directions, deep into the crowd.

17

As soon as I returned to the High Commission, I rang Emma.

"Nick, I dreamed about what happened on the boat, dreamed it was me..."

"I thought it was you. Try to forget it. An awful... coincidence. Look, about Robert..." I told her about the meeting with IF. "The good news is that he's alive. I believe that."

"What's the bad news?" she asked in a low voice.

I hesitated. "The demands are... difficult to meet."

"You mean, impossible."

I did mean impossible or almost, but I couldn't say it. "Well, there may be a lot we can do to find Robert. We may have some tangible leads from today."

Emma remained quiet for a moment. "Tangible leads, huh? It's as if he's dead now, in a way..."

"Keep hoping. There's a lot we can do."

"I'm glad to hear that. Not too much seems to have been done so far, though. What's so impossible about the demands?"

"Releasing terrorists. HMG and Pakistan won't be blackmailed. That's the policy, anyway."

"Oh, they call it blackmail. If they wanted to do it, they'd call it a deal– an exchange. What did you mean about coincidence just now?"

"You and Macbeth."

"God, that's a sick thought. I've talked to Gerry, heart to heart. He doesn't hold anything against me. We're friends, don't you understand, Nick? I really like him. He knows that. I suppose I owe him, but it's a debt that's no problem to pay. He's so nice."

"You've got it completely wrong, Emma," I retorted, choking on the line, unable to express what I felt with a telephone in my hand.

Emma was silent for a moment. "It doesn't sound like much of a demand to me, what the terrorists are asking."

"The captives they want released are very dangerous men."

"Well, that's that, then," Emma said with a sob, and rang off.

I rang back but she didn't answer. I stayed on the line for a time. I wanted to talk about the video tape of Robert.

Annoyed and confused, I went to report to Grace Stewart.

"Come in, Nick," she said, packing papers into her briefcase. "I'm going back to the Hilton. I've heard from Dennis Robbins. It's awful. And you got a tape."

"Yes, Robert being brave."

"Do you think that's why it hasn't been fed to Al Jazira TV?"

A very short video, which Robbins and I had viewed in his office on the way back, showed Robert sitting before a black sheet covered in slogans, his legs bound at the ankles. A hooded man with a rifle was nudging him with the barrel. Robert was frowning disdainfully, his lips mouthing oaths. He held an English language newspaper in his hand so that the date was visible.

"Defiance isn't much use to the IF," I said.

"He is, as you say, a brave man."

I watched her check the files as she continued to pack her briefcase. When she had finished, she snapped the case shut and locked it with a small key. "Departmental regulations, you know," she smiled, slipping the key in her pocket.

"You're a cool one," I said, blocking the door as she smoothed her jacket and picked up the briefcase.

"What do you mean?" she said, reverting to the role of boss.

"For Christ's sake, the Special Envoy is under sentence of death and you're tripping off to your hotel to have a shower!"

"Don't be sexist, Mr Dyson. It's 6.30pm. I've worked a long day. I'm going to my hotel to continue. I'm not tripping anywhere!" The Scots accent was much more pronounced now.

"The point is: Robert Laidlaw is going to die unless you do something," I said harshly.

She gently placed her briefcase on the floor by the desk and returned to her chair. "Sit down. There is a misunderstanding here. We must talk."

"Misunderstanding, my ass," I said quietly, continuing to stand.

"As far as I'm concerned, the investigation into Sir Robert's kidnapping is being handled perfectly ably by Special Branch, the local police and, in particular, Dennis Robbins. My job is to lead the mission. I'm not a policeman."

"Balls."

"We won't get far, Nick, unless you are rational. I know it's a shock for you. I know Sir Robert is your friend. But there's no point in being abusive."

"Spare me the conventional reactions. Let's have some straight talk for a change. This is political stuff, Grace. We can obtain the release of Ali and Mussafa and pick them up later. You advise the government on this."

"I do and the advice to government is clear. We don't surrender to terrorists– not even at the cost of the life of an ambassador."

"That's what the copybook may say, but prisoner trades have been made before. You could press this with the government and with Pakistan."

Grace shook her head negatively.

"You won't do it– not even go through the motions?"

"No point."

"And we're not making an all-out attempt to get to Robert. Not the half-baked show Robbins is putting on. We should at least make some kind of promise to comply, so we can delay and get close to the IF and snatch Robert."

"I can't do anything about that," Grace said, matter-of-factly, tapping her fingernails on the polished wood of the desk impatiently.

"You can! That's exactly what I mean. You could get FO authorisation to talk to the Pakistan Government about exchange. Even if it doesn't come off, the word will be out that we're trying and we will have time to get closer to the IF. You can get Hall to beef up the investigating team. You can insist on the team proceeding according to a known plan, instead of groping around for inspiration while we watch the butterflies in the Residence garden."

Grace stood, slowly and deliberately, and picked up her bag. "I can't say any more to you."

As she came from behind the desk, I grasped her arm. She was looking straight at me. "Could it be that it's not in your interest to try too hard?"

"That is absurd," she said, going past me to the door. She turned on the threshold. "I suggest you resign immediately.

I don't want you with me. You've got your emotions confused with the job. Have your letter on my desk first thing in the morning. I'll expedite it."

As she walked out I sprang after her, catching her arm again.

"Get your hands off!"

"Listen," I said, forcing her to halt, "the last thing I'm going to do is resign. I'm going to stay close to the so-called investigation; and if you try to get rid of me, watch out for yourself!"

My eyes caught hers for a second, just long enough for me to see a spark of concern. She was a true careerist who followed every rule, and now she had been threatened on a personal level in the biggest assignment of her career. She wasn't used to the roughhouse.

I went down to the Pilot's Bar and had a quiet beer. I'd alarmed her and she deserved it.

18

I sat up in bed in my apartment, with a cigar, a brandy, a pencil and an A4 pad at hand. I wanted to note what I could do to find Robert. I couldn't recline on the lawn of the Residence as a spectator any more. I wanted to do something.

After fifteen minutes of chewing the pencil, my list was short. The brandy was gone, leaving the bitterness of strong tobacco on my tongue. On the side marked 'Unfriendly', I had Leighton, Grace, Bradshaw, Hall and Robbins. All of them knew more than I did and were certainly not being frank with me. I was allowed to meetings because I was Robert's puppy dog. It had the appearance of being consultative and looked right on paper. However, I had come to believe that they were all pursuing their own agendas while dabbling in the search. They were not wicked; they were just self-interested and selfish, like me.

Under the heading 'Other people', I jotted down Emma. She might have a clue about the mistress, the woman in the Sheraton video– if they were the same person. The woman in the video certainly seemed to be involved. It was difficult to think that her purpose in being with Robert and entering the murder room was merely a love tryst.

Robbins had told me he had identified the man in the video, but not the woman. Photo recognition had identified him as Ghafoor Khan, who had spent five years in custody in India for political crimes. He had been released a year ago. He wasn't specifically known to be implicated with IF. Robbins had given me a copy of Khan's official record, which I now had with me. He was a clerk when he was employed. Some short employments were listed but it struck me to see that he had worked for Macbeth Docks as a clerk for five years. Another connection. I had the thought that somebody like him could be the bridge between the IF and Macbeth.

Then, I wrote 'Sheraton staff'. The partly missing security video raised questions in itself. Against that item, I added: 'No language capability.' It was impossible for me to do what would have been easy in Britain: wander into the hotel, buttonhole staff members quietly and ask a lot of questions.

I listed a new item: 'Rashida and HC staff'. Rashida had been prickly when I had pressed her on who Robert had left the building with. She knew something. I could also talk to the security staff and the tea-makers.

Under the heading 'Documentary and computer sources', I noted confidential and secret files. My access to these was severely limited and only available through Grace. I marked this heading with a big X. However, I did scribble 'Unofficial access?' because it was worth thinking about. It would mean breaking a few rules, but so what? My career here without Robert was finished.

Finally, I circled Rashida's name with my pencil several times. It stood out, beyond all the others, as the most tangible starting point for me. However, I could clear another avenue first. I refreshed my brandy and dialled Emma's number. She was out.

I reached Emma on the telephone after breakfast the next morning.

"What on earth do you want at this hour, Nick? I've got the most God-awful hangover, darling. I really can't think."

I had the usual pang of jealousy but concealed it. When I asked if she knew any way of finding out the name of Robert's woman friend, Emma became chilly.

"I thought there was a bitch sniffing around," she said, "but I was only guessing. Not very inspired guesswork."

"Is there any woman whom he was associated with for official reasons that might, just might, have been more than that?"

"Only every good-looking fuckable woman in Islamabad."

It was a dumb question and I gave up the enquiry, convinced that she knew nothing helpful. When I arrived at the Commission, I made a detour on my way to my office by passing Robert's. His room led off a quiet tiled hall with muted lights and old etchings of trade on the Indus. I found Rashida at her desk. She was working for Grace Stewart. Fortunately, there was nobody else about. I told her how worried I was, then pulled up a chair on her side of the desk and lowered my voice.

"Do you think we could have a chat about that day? Even the smallest thing you remember might be important." I deliberately made my request sound ambiguous, as though I was interested in talking to her for herself.

Rashida looked up at me more than sympathetically. She was dressed with her usual care in a tight floral dress, which was cool and plain, and had a low neckline. She liked to display her cleavage prominently, unperturbed by the mores of her half-country. Her skin was a smooth gold, and her jet-black hair was lacquered and piled high like a guardsman's beaver. Her wide eyes caressed me.

"I can't talk to you here," she said, archly.

"Come to my office when you're free." I tried to be as enticing as possible.

"I'll see," she said, with a pretence of casualness, returning to her keyboard.

Half an hour later, I had my head in my hands and was staring down at a piece of notepaper. I was trying to calculate whether I should approach Grace about our row last night and what I should say. I heard a knock and Rashida put her head around the door with a grin.

"OK?" she whispered conspiratorially.

I jumped up and went forward, closing the door behind her. I took her hands in mine and drew her close, smelling her scent.

"Be a good boy," she said, easing me away but radiating pleasure.

"It's very important to identify this woman in the video," I said, as we took seats on each side of the desk. "Rashida, I understand that you are a loyal secretary, but the best loyalty at the moment is to tell what you know."

"I haven't seen the video."

"I'll arrange it."

Rashida fixed me with a glance, sitting erect with her breasts thrust out. If I looked hard at the thin material of her dress, I could see two dark circles around the prominent outline of her nipples. They seemed mysterious rather than sexy.

"I'm only helping you, Nick, because I trust you…" she paused, her grainy voice dropping, "and I like you. It's not going to take things any further, but I do know the name of the woman who left here with Sir Robert. It was Celia Abdali from the Health Commission."

"Did you tell the police?"

"They didn't ask me."

The name meant nothing to me, but I felt a start of annoyance at the incompetence of Robbins' investigation. "Was it Robbins you spoke to?"

"No, I don't think so. It was two of his men."

"Can I ask how you know Celia Abdali?"

"I don't. She's a high-class Pakistani woman. I've seen her here. I've taken notes at her meetings with Sir Hugh. She's on the Pakistan Medical Board. I doubt if she could have had anything to do with Sir Robert's abduction."

She sounded to me like the kind of woman Robert would have charmed at official cocktail parties. "Were they having an affair?"

"I don't know," Rashida simpered lustfully, delighted at the thought. "She used to ring him, sometimes three or four times in a day and then not for a week."

I wondered why Robbins hadn't identified Celia Abdali, if she was the woman in the video, and why the questioning of Rashida had been so lax. As I walked to the door with Rashida, I anticipated that she was expecting a reward for being cooperative. An affectionate gesture might do it. I let my hand stray down to the small of her back.

"Nick," she said, stopping to face me. "I go bowling with the girls on Thursday evenings at the Sun Centre at 7 pm... I don't have to, you know?"

I thought for a moment, genuinely trying to find a way out of what felt like a duty. If I was busy on a Thursday, she'd only find another day. I had encouraged her approach and I didn't want to offend her. As Grace's temporary secretary, she could be of use to me.

"OK. Thursday, 7.30 pm outside the Centre."

I sounded bright and pressed my palm a little more firmly against her lower– very much lower– back to reassure her. Just then, there was a single knock at the door, which opened simultaneously. Grace stood in the doorway.

"Thank you, Mr Dyson," Rashida said, and walked out of the room past Grace.

"Excuse me," Grace said to me.

Grace had seen it: the disposition of two bodies and the facial expressions. Her intuition had told her. Rather than let her score a point, or a further point, I launched into an attack before she sat down.

"I've thought it over, Grace, what I said last night and I meant it. I'm staying until the Laidlaw affair is finished. If you try to get rid of me, you'll get trouble with a capital T. If I have to, I'll take my case to Westminster. Any claim that there's a government screw-up will involve Robert's political friends. There'll be an enquiry. Dirt will tarnish you because you're the boss." I spoke in a moderate tone. This prediction went far beyond my real intentions, but Grace would never know that.

Grace summoned an open-eyed, ultra-frank expression, but I could see that her breathing movement was more rapid than usual. She had absorbed the implications of my threat. "I only came to tell you to forget what I said about resigning. So your outburst is unnecessary."

"Don't view it as an outburst, Grace. I mean what I say. I want a proper investigation. If you or anybody else lets up on the search for Robert, for whatever reason, I'll make a lot of trouble."

"Let's try to work together, Nick. I respect what you're trying to do for Sir Robert. It's what we're all trying to do in our own way."

Her career was too important to her to battle openly with me. It was true that I could cast a slur on her reputation. She must have realised this by the time she got back to her hotel last night. The blue stains under her eyes suggested one too many gins from the minibar.

I was aware, too, of my vulnerability. Even though Grace couldn't fire me outright – she had no case and wouldn't get away with it, and I didn't think she had the nerve – but she could use the tried and trusted ways of the civil service to remove a bolshie assistant with three years to run on his employment contract. She'd privately and delicately dump on me in every official memo she could while building up her indictment, which would eventually be revealed: disregard of policy, emotionalism, abuse of senior staff, inappropriate behaviour with female staff, etc. Surely but slowly.

Grace needed months. She couldn't afford to have me complaining about her in the meantime. She had to appear to make friends. Since I planned to ditch the job long before she was ready to press my exit button, I didn't care. I was thinking of weeks of employment, not years, if Robert didn't return. If he did, it would be a different story.

"I've forgotten what you said about resigning," I said pleasantly, "but don't forget what I said about your responsibility to get the investigation into gear."

"We've heard each other," she said in her detached way, then walked out.

19

I reached Robbins on the phone in his office and explained my detective work on Celia Abdali. He listened in silence.

"How did you learn this?"

"By doing what you should have done: making enquiries among HC staff."

"I think you can leave it to me, Nick."

"Did you know that Dr Abdali could be involved?"

Robbins hesitated. "I don't think she is involved. She's a respectable civil servant."

"I asked if you knew."

"One of my subordinates questioned Rashida Masood."

"I asked if you knew Abdali could be involved. You saw the video. A hundred top people could identify her. I expect you could, too."

"Look, Nick, I'm the investigator here, as I've had to say to you before."

"I'll take that as a 'yes'."

"Don't. I'm not accountable to you."

"Why the cover-up?"

Robbins emitted a small gasp of pretended amusement. "I'm not covering anything up!"

"Are you going to get photo identification of Abdali and compare it with the woman on the video?"

Robbins was breathing heavily. "Yes, I'm doing that."

"You haven't done it already?" When Robbins didn't

answer promptly, I said, "You already know the video woman is Abdali, don't you?"

"I said I'd check."

Robbins would have hung up the receiver if protocol allowed him to show his feelings and I wasn't going to let him off. "Any trace on the IF?"

"No."

"Your people lost the trail? You don't have a lot of luck, do you?"

"One thing I'll tell you, Nick, since you seem to want to pick over the details. You remember that flask that the IF handed over at our meeting? I noticed that there seemed to be something inside it. It made a faint noise when I shook the flask. It wasn't liquid. It was a small piece of paper that had been torn from the margin of a newspaper. Took a lot of fishing out. It had one word scratched on it: 'Macbeth.'"

My chest thumped. "What did that mean to you?"

"It wasn't a reference to Shakespeare and not a familiar name around here. I assumed it meant that Gerald Macbeth had information that could help us. I went to see him."

"What did he say?"

"He couldn't understand why Sir Robert would have written his name – if he did– and he knew nothing other than what he'd read in the papers."

"Well, Dennis," I spoke as warmly as I could, trying to reciprocate his friendliness in letting me know this new piece of information– "what it means to me is that Macbeth is behind this."

"That is… stupid."

"Macbeth hates Robert. They have a history. Somebody set Robert up at the hotel. Macbeth is in that frame."

"That is verging on the… looney."

"If the woman who walked down the corridor with Ghafoor Khan, an ex-convict with connections to terrorists, is Abdali, then big establishment people are involved in Robert's disappearance."

"You're not making any sense to me, Nick."

"We'll see if I'm making sense when we know whether the woman in the video is Abdali."

I finished the call convinced that Macbeth's role was now beyond any doubt. The full impact of Robbins's evasiveness struck me. And why shouldn't I go directly to Abdali myself? I thought about calling her for an hour, then I picked up the phone and asked the operator for the Health Commission. I was put through to Dr Abdali. I didn't think it would be that easy. She came on the line with a low, Americanised voice, not one I would have associated with the elegant Eastern woman in the video.

"This is Nicholas Dyson, Robert Laidlaw's assistant."

She sounded surprised.

"I know you are a friend of Robert's. I was wondering if we could meet. You might be able to help me."

"Who? What?" she replied, her voice turning harsh. "Just one minute."

She went off the line and it went dead. I dialled back and was put through to the operator who had taken the previous call. "I'm sorry, Dr Abdali is not available."

"But I was speaking to her a moment ago on this line."

"I'm sorry. She's not here now. She's very busy. Would you like to leave your name and number?"

20

It was nearly 11am, time for the meeting with Grace Stewart before seeing the Pakistan Trade Association delegation. They were representing the contractors who were putting on pressure for reinstatement contracts for two bridges in Iraq, and an airfield and several roads in Afghanistan. Robert had enjoyed being wined and dined by them, but they hadn't fooled him. 'They're just a sophisticated version of the pirates their forbears were,' he'd said. 'The same as their brothers in the mountains. I wouldn't call them crooks – well, not precisely. They have pens in their hands instead of Kalashnikovs.'

When I asked Robert if he had met Macbeth at these meetings, he had said, 'Not face to face. He's never been present at any of our dinners or negotiations.'

'But he's listed as the deputy head.'

'If he wants to keep out of the way, it's not a problem.'

'It's significant though, isn't it?'

'Only to a paranoid character like you, Nick. Don't worry so much!'

I went to Grace's office and she barely greeted me. Bradshaw caught my eye privately with a movement of the eyebrow that indicated Grace was out of sorts. Apparently, she hadn't cooled from our last exchange.

Grace passed round a note on Howard Chunagar, one of the leaders of the Karachi business community, as well as a barrister and a millionaire in shipping and property. I had already met him before and again at the reception for Grace Stewart's arrival. He was a member of a number of government councils and came from an old and respected local family.

One name I expected to find on Grace's list made me uneasy: Gerald Macbeth. She dwelt on Macbeth. "He's young, very rich and powerful. In his own right his company– or should I say his father's company, of which he now has control, is one of the biggest companies in Pakistan, and a blue chip in the financial market."

I didn't reveal that I knew Macbeth, but instead felt a twinge of envy at this modern tycoon who had enough weight to make it felt in the government of a foreign land. The envy quickly turned to a feeling of distaste at the thought of having to confront him. This distaste came down to the fact that in comparison, my own position was so damn menial and with Robert's disappearance, almost irrelevant.

We covered the background of the other members of the delegation quickly: relations of wealthy families, who had leeched on Pakistan society for generations, and European representatives of international engineering contractors. It was evident that Grace didn't intend to discuss with us the line she would be taking at the meeting or any substantive issues. Madam would reveal all in due course. Bradshaw and I were expected to sit like dummies and just give information if requested.

The meeting was within walking distance of the High Commission in a government council room It was like an English local authority chamber in teak and dark blue leather, with pretentious carved wood cornices and various levels of seating. We took our seats at a long and wide table in the central well of the chamber. A row of businessmen in immaculate suits and with groomed hair were already seated opposite; they exuded ease and confidence and greeted us in a quiet and friendly way as we all settled down over our papers.

I was virtually eyeball to eyeball with Gerald Macbeth. He had lost some hair from his temples and his close-fitting suit accentuated his wide shoulders and long body. His face was sallow and hollow-cheeked, and his eyes flamed. This was the man that fascinated Emma. I had to concede that his devilish looks would be attractive to a woman. Perhaps there was some Portugese, Pakistani or even a touch of Chinese in Macbeth's lineage. Despite our proximity, though, we never exchanged a glance– let alone any sign of recognition. It needn't have been like this. Was I being small-minded? I should have greeted him heartily as an old school friend, but he wasn't a friend. He was an undeclared enemy. I could have dismissed the past as something trivial and offered my hand, but the past wasn't trivial. I had been the unwitting agent of his downfall, or one of the agents. I feared what his reaction to me would be if I attempted to make a connection.

Grace recorded the tragic absence of Sir Robert Laidlaw and introduced us. She said we were there to learn the viewpoint of the Association and then handed over to Howard Chunagar.

He shortly regretted the absence of Sir Robert and talked as though we were all on the same side. He said it was only a matter of making the British Government understand what huge investments Pakistan companies had made in Iraq and Afghanistan, and how mutually valuable the commercial ties with Britain were.

"We agree and we're doing everything we can to take those trade ties forward," Grace said.

"Well," Chunagar said, "I hope not in the way that Sir Robert had in mind. I wish he was here because we feel he has given unfair preference to some companies who have secured big contracts."

"I can't imagine Sir Robert doing that--" Grace said.

"Oh, yes, and he gave us assurances that have turned out to be worthless."

Bradshaw leaned towards me and said, "Get it? They think it's their turn to be preferred."

Macbeth broke into the pause, a vein pulsing in his long neck. "We have reason to think that Laidlaw was financially involved with his favoured companies."

"That's… a very serious allegation," Grace Stewart said.

My shiver of concern at being found with what might be identified as bribe money was stifled by wrath. Perhaps Robert had heaped one more indignity on Macbeth by ignoring Macbeth Docks. "Sir Robert isn't here to defend himself so that's an unacceptable allegation," I said.

I was breaking the unwritten rule that one should only speak when spoken to, but I wasn't going to listen to this sleek, predatory entrepreneur who was traducing Robert.

Grace turned to me in agitation, but I had Chunagar's eye and had added a fresh impetus to the meeting. "You better tell us what the details are and what the source of your information is," I said.

"We've made all our information available to Special Branch. Leonard Hall is aware," Macbeth rejoined smoothly, with a complacent scowl.

"Tell us one scrap of evidence that supports what you say," I challenged.

"This is not the place," Macbeth relied in a triumphantly melodious voice. The timbre of the voice and the superior tone travelled up from the dark of years gone by.

Bradshaw had his plump palm covering his lower face. He was highly amused. Two red spots were visible on Grace's normally creamy cheeks. I was hardened by the fact that Hall and therefore Grace knew more about the allegation than I did.

"Then it's wrong to make such allegations at all. You either withdraw them until justified by the police, or produce evidence. You can't expect us to consult while you defame the absent senior British representative."

Chunagar gave a confused smile. The rest of his group remained poker-faced, except for Macbeth who showed a savage satisfaction.

"I think we should remember that it's an allegation that requires investigation and put it from our minds while we discuss our business," Chunagar said softly.

"Laidlaw is corrupt," Macbeth said harshly.

"Withdraw that, please," I replied. "Mr Chunagar, please call on your deputy to withdraw that!" I could see I was driving into a brick wall.

"Never," Macbeth said, shaking his head emphatically.

I swung around to Grace, whose cheeks were burning in her white face. "I believe we should withdraw, Grace. This is an intolerable insult."

Grace looked down at the mirror surface of the table and muttered, "I am in charge of this delegation. We will continue."

"Very well," I said. "Excuse me." I stood up as calmly as I could, picked up my file and walked out, but not before I heard Macbeth snigger.

21

I left the meeting knowing I was heading for another battle with Grace, as well as a certain reprimand and suspension if she was prepared to brave my threats. Confused as my feelings for Robert were, I couldn't have sat through the meeting. The old loyalties that stirred in me were vitriolically alive after all this time. I reflected that the wars of the March House days were childish and petty games in hindsight, but at the time they were campaigns for conquest as real as the pig-fest for contracts in Iraq and Afghanistan.

Macbeth had mounted a small reprisal for the damage he suffered from Emma and from me: the pleasure of openly branding Robert as corrupt. I hated (and feared) Macbeth, but I couldn't blame him. What concerned me more is what Macbeth might have done to Robert and what he might do to me and Emma, yet.

I was burning to talk to Emma about the meeting with Macbeth and I arranged to visit her that evening. I thought, at first, that she was more worried about Robert than I had realised. She put her arms around me for a moment at the door of the apartment and then led me into her smartly furnished lounge.

"Hugh Leighton called me and told me about the meeting with Robert's captors. And the video. I don't want to see it myself. It's too horrible. And he's given me a guard, too— a plain-clothes man."

"I know, I spotted him on the way in."

"Do you think I'm in danger, Nick?"

"I doubt it. I think the old man's being very cautious, that's all. Look, I met Macbeth today at a business function." An evasive look, almost of amusement, passed across her face.

"Emma, he never showed any sign of recognition."

She shrugged. "I can imagine he doesn't think much of you, but that's nothing to do with me."

"I know he's a big financial success," I said, "but do you think what happened in England affected his repute here?"

"Not a sausage! Who's worried about what happened in England ten or fifteen years ago? Gerry spends most of his time in Australia and the US when he's not here. I think he's put it all behind him."

She was prancing before me, beautiful, confident, excited at the mention of Macbeth's name. Thoughts of her husband were now minimal in her mind.

"It's wishful thinking that he's put it behind him, Emma."

"Why should you think anything different, Nick?"

I had felt the effect of the man's baleful stare a few hours earlier. If ever there was malevolence, Macbeth projected it as though the injury had been suffered yesterday.

"At the meeting he accused Robert of taking bribes to allocate contracts. It was malicious and unnecessary, far beyond…"

Emma didn't seem disturbed, and she certainly didn't want to defend her husband. "Maybe Robert did take bribes, although, God knows, we always seemed to be hard up."

The thought that Emma was about to embark on a new phase with Macbeth stirred turbulent feelings in me.

"I'm not saying I'm doing anything with Gerry, but what if I did?" She spoke provocatively, relishing my disquiet.

"Don't you see?"

"I don't see anything but a very attractive and rich man who wants me."

"The past makes it impossible."

"Oh, fiddle about the past! What do I care? What does anybody care?"

"Do you seriously think he could forget what you did to him, dragging him into court, months of agony, of worry, shattering his reputation and ruining his promise?"

"Oh, it's not as bad as you say and it was years ago!" she said, trying to appear at ease and clapping her hands in dismissal.

I could see a shaft of self-doubt in her look, though. Part of me appreciated that she was a trivial, perhaps silly woman, but she was in my bloodstream. "I love you, Emma," I said, grabbing her roughly and kissing her. "Let's get away from all this. Let's go back to England now– tomorrow!"

"My, what a he-man you are, Nick," she said, liking it. "But you hardly have a buck to your name, unless that money I saw you with recently is yours… no, you're honest and reliable. I know that. Anyway, I'm beginning to rather like it here. It's a fun place. I don't want to go back to cold old Blighty."

"You seem to think that by offering your body, you can banish the wrong."

"Nick, you're jealous! Don't try and dress it up that Gerry is going to do me a mortal injury, because it's rubbish. It's the reverse. I'm making up for the past. He cares for me."

So she was having an affair with Macbeth! I choked inside, unable to press her any further. I suppressed my concerns and tried for an hour to be the amusing person she liked over drinks. Then, when she was mellow, I made love to her.

At Kashif Gap afterwards, I poured myself a large tumbler of whisky and dropped in two ice cubes. For perhaps fifteen or twenty minutes I would be able to think painfully straight and then it would all recede in a fuzz.

I took my usual seat on the terrace. It was nearly 2am and the lawns below were quiet and dark. I recalled the pall of scandal that had hung over Poole Abbey in the months before the trial. The newspapers had billed the affair The Public School Rape; and although there was a limit to what they could say before the trial, they all promised a feast of revelations about the degenerate lifestyle of public schoolboys and their wealthy parents. The only bright spot had been Laidlaw who had been jubilant. His rival had been removed and he would go on to become head of house.

22

By accident, I was a major participant in the infliction of an injury to Gerald Macbeth, which had wounded him to the core of his mind and, I believe, scarred him for life.

It was the night of the annual sixth form dance with the Poole Abbey Girls' School. To the masters, at least, it was a restrained affair, and took place in the school hall. Teachers from both schools provided plenty of chaperones. Before the ball, tuxedo-clad sixth-formers had an awkward sherry in the housemaster's study with their partners before walking down the hill to the hall.

The night was warm for autumn. Most of the boys, who should have been in bed or doing their prep, were preparing for a few hours of freedom while the masters and senior boys were away. This was a night for drinking, poker, grudge fights and raids on neighbouring schoolhouses.

I was too junior to attend the ball this year and was instead with two friends behind the trees on the lawn, enjoying a beer. My companions went back to the house. I was about to follow, but I took a few minutes to finish my cigarette and enjoy the freedom.

The darkness was not complete. The windows of the house were 50 feet away; on the ground floor, some of them were open. A few lights were on. I suddenly heard a sound. At first, I thought it was a cat or a fox in the shrubbery, but then the low moan turned into a sob. It was coming from the house. The sob had a frightening urgency; it was a human sound. Then, there was a scream– a short, clear, penetrating female scream.

I stepped behind the trunk of the oak tree that brooded over the garden, alarmed that I was going to be called upon to act in some way. After a moment I saw a figure emerge from the windows and quickly disappear into the deeper shadows of the cloister. I recognised the longish head with a high pile of dark hair: Gerald Macbeth. That was all; a glance of a few seconds that would change our lives. I thought nothing of it at the time.

I entered the house and played several hands of blackjack and poker with my friends in the dormitory By the time I had done so, my future had taken an unexpected turn in a way that I could never have anticipated. I was not alone in having heard the scream. Stories accumulated in the dormitories that night, different accounts, from different sets of eyes and ears, were knitted, rightly or wrongly, into a coherent thread of narrative that materialised in the common room the next morning.

Robin Lovelace, a junior Latin master fresh from Cambridge, had been on duty and had gone to the assistant matron's room as soon as he had heard the scream. When he had flicked on the lights he had found Emma Southern crying and with a red-blue swelling on her cheek. He had then taken her to his room and called the headmaster and the housemaster; shortly after, they had come puffing up the hill in their bow ties, purpled and disturbed.

The headmaster then called the school doctor and, after consulting him, the police. A long discussion behind closed doors ensued. Emma was driven to her parents' home by the headmaster. The Southerns were a prominent local family. Her father had been an MP and was a Poole Abbey governor. Emma, his youngest child, had finished school and was helping at Poole Abbey before going to an art course at an academy in London.

These were the 'facts' that were shared by us boys on the morning after, thanks to our collective efforts at detective work.

I was distraught. The girl I loved had been brutalised. The boys were tense and excited as the police and masters had sought the culprit. I, alone, knew who had done it. I could have killed Macbeth. I had no intention of telling the masters or the police, though. Omerta was the rule. I intended to take revenge personally. It was natural that I should go to Laidlaw to get advice and support. His expression was incredulous at first, then determined.

"You must tell the police, Dyson, you little worm!"

"That's crazy. We can deal with Macbeth ourselves."

For a person who scorned all authority, especially the police, Robert was icily adamant. "If you don't tell Policeman Plod the vision that came before your piggy eyes, Dyson, I'll tell him you're withholding evidence of a serious crime."

"I'm not talking." It was the only time then or since that I flatly refused Robert.

He went to Larsen's office. When he came out, he called two of his trusties; they grabbed me and manhandled me into Larsen's room. Larsen rose ponderously from his chair.

"Talk, Dyson!" Robert shouted.

I remember Larsen's sickly stare. "If you know something of this wretched business, Dyson, you must tell me."

I stood mute until, after half a minute or so, Larsen said he would hand me over to the police. I gave in.

My statement to the police clinched Macbeth's arrest. Waxy little ears glued to keyholes also concluded that Emma, too, had named Macbeth. He was arrested, taken to the cells was and later charged with rape and assault.

23

Macbeth was in disgrace for months. He was allowed to return to Pakistan on a huge bond, his fine academic potential in tatters. In just a few months, a godlike young man with every gift had been reduced to a nervous wreck with his freedom at risk. Even the finest lawyers in England couldn't prevent the pain and the threat.

When the trial eventually started at Salisbury Crown Court, I was summoned to attend and was taken to the court in a police car. But none of these frills on the life of a schoolboy made it a welcome outing. The only good thing was that I would have a chance to see Emma, who had seemingly vanished since the night of the crime. I glimpsed her outside the court in the company of a firm-faced old woman with a posy of styled grey hair and spectacles, presumably her mother. Emma gave me a wan smile.

"Hello. Dyson, isn't it?" she said. My chest heaved.

She looked striking but pale in a black costume. A cop murmured that she couldn't speak to witnesses and shepherded her and the woman away. I was confined to the witnesses' room during the hearing, sitting in miserable silence alongside people in other cases.

I was allowed out at lunchtime. I saw Emma walking away from the court and then parting from the older woman. I had been warned not to talk to anybody about the case, but I ignored it and followed her. I came up beside her. She seemed pleased. We talked trivia about the school for a few moments until she stopped, tears in her eyes. "I don't want to go on with this!" she said. We halted on the footpath of a narrow street lined with shops. People streamed past us.

"I never wanted it either," I said.

She looked at me accusingly. "Then why did you tell the police you saw Macbeth?"

"I did see him! I wasn't going to talk. The prefects made me. They dragged me into Larsen's office and threatened to hand me over to the police."

To my surprise, she put her hand on my arm sympathetically. "It was the same with me. I was forced, Dyson. The police, the headmaster, my father. The doctor said I had injuries consistent with rape– you know, lacerations. And my arms and face were bruised. What could I say? I had no idea there'd be a case in court. Then it started to roll forward like a damn tank, crushing Gerry and me!"

"I guess you had to tell the police," I said.

"God! You've got no idea how the headmaster and Larsen carried on that night about the disgrace to the school. I think they'd rather have buried me in the garden than report it. Then, when the doctor saw me and said I was telling the truth, they made me tell who…"

I felt the process we were in was inexorable.

"How can I stop it, Dyson?" It was a cry of agony.

I thought for a moment. "You could say you were half knocked out and confused…" My thin invention frittered away.

However, she took me seriously, and the tears in her eyes receded, replaced instead by a sharper look. "They'll want to know who the somebody else was."

"Just say it was a stranger."

"Don't be silly, Dyson," she said, stepping away from

me as though I was being obtuse. "You know there was somebody else."

"Who?" I said, astounded at her look of complicity.

"The person who put you up to giving evidence against Macbeth."

"Emma, I saw Macbeth."

"Christ!" she said, "He didn't do anything."

Nudged and buffeted by the passing crowd, we edged down a side street to a bench by the footpath. The case was one of those events that happened in the world of adults. You were supposed to understand and you thought you did, but some unknown essential piece was left out of your picture and suddenly you didn't understand at all. And it was alarming when you found you didn't understand.

"You've got to unravel this, Emma."

"How in the name of God can I do it?" she cried and fell into my arms, sobbing.

My lips touched the skin of her cheek. I was in my grey serge Poole Abbey suit and school tie. It was the most heart-bursting moment of my life.

24

The day after the meeting with Macbeth, I wanted to see what progress Robbins had made with Celia Abdali. I called Special Branch and reached Robbins at 9am.

"Have you identified the woman on the tape?"

"Yes, we were able to do that from employment records at the Health Commission."

"It's taken you a hell of a long time. She's consorting with terrorists. She's involved."

"Don't jump to conclusions. I'm having difficulty getting hold of her."

"Why is she like this?" I asked, remembering her treatment of me and thinking that it confirmed her entanglement.

"Embarrassed, I'd say."

"Embarrassed! So where do you go from here?"

"I think we're wasting our time. This woman may have been involved with Sir Robert, but she can't have anything to do with his abduction."

"Why?"

"She's a public servant of high reputation."

"You're telling me a witness who was at the crime scene, consorting with a convicted terrorist, is ruled out because you think she's innocent– without even interviewing her?"

"I've arranged to see her this afternoon."

"Why haven't you got to her before now? Why didn't you question Rashida Masood personally?"

"I've told you, Nick. Look, if it will satisfy you, come along with me."

His sudden change of tack surprised me and I decided not to harry him any further. "OK, Dennis."

I now had to face an angry Grace Stewart. Rashida had been leaving message notes in my office since 8.30am. When I went into Grace's office I could see she was still stewing. Her hands were clenched in front of her and the red blotches on her cheeks were as they had been in the meeting. Her natural complexion was pale, which accentuated the colour spots even further.

"You and I can't work together like this," she said, superficially composed.

"When the head of this mission is insulted by a bunch of profiteers on the make, I'd expect our leader to defend him. You were prepared to sit there in the name of diplomacy and let them say what they felt like saying," I said, quietly.

"I'm taking the lead in the talks and I'll decide what's to be said and when; and I'll say, it unless I ask for your help."

"I'm still on the team, then?" I asked, not caring much about the answer.

It was a very low-key rebuke. Grace was sufficiently wary of me not to even talk tough. "For the time being," she said, with distaste.

"Did you eventually withdraw yesterday?"

"Yes, but not in good shape. I would have dealt with Macbeth. I thought he was out of order. You made me look a fool."

I knew she wanted to kick me out, but she was even more worried about me making a fuss. This was the rift in her well-assumed calm. I had a hold on her.

I did a little work that morning preparing papers for Grace– details of infrastructure work required in Iraq and Afghanistan– but my mind was on the evasive Dr Abdali. At noon I walked down to the Hilton coffee shop, had a sandwich and a beer and then asked my driver to take me to the Health Commission. I might have walked but I wanted to arrive cool, and to have an air-conditioned sanctuary outside the building in which to wait for Robbins. A High Commission car pulled up on time and let Robbins out. I caught him up at the top of the steps to the entrance.

"Don't forget me, will you? I can't resist a beautiful woman."

"This is a police enquiry," Robbins snapped.

"I'm good enough to see poor old Petrie and the terrorists, but when it comes to the ladies..."

Robbins looked at me acrimoniously and went to the enquiry desk. A big, bald, black man with a gleaming head and heavily rimmed spectacles, spent a long time enigmatically tapping a computer keyboard and looking calmly at the screen. Eventually, he told Robbins to wait and he attended to another enquiry.

"Why don't you tell him this is a police enquiry by appointment?" I asked Robbins impatiently.

"I have to be discreet."

"Discreet? Shit, you should have police here with an arrest warrant!"

Robbins parleyed with the attendant for a second time and we were admitted. We climbed two flights of dark stairs and found Dr Abdali's secretary's room. It was crammed with columns of manila files set on top of each other. The piles climbed crankily up the walls as high as one could reach and threatened to progress out of the door into the dark corridor. In the centre of this mess a Pakistani woman in an orange headscarf sat before a computer.

She stood up for us and smiled. "I'm sorry, Dr Abdali isn't here."

"We have an appointment," Robbins said.

The woman merely smiled.

"Do you have a record of the appointment?" I asked.

She turned and flipped a few pages of a big notebook. "No."

"Do you understand this is a police enquiry?" I said.

"Please…" Robbins said.

The woman watched, silent and composed.

"When will Dr Abdali be back?" he asked.

"Not today."

"Tomorrow?"

"I can't be sure."

Robbins and I retired in disarray and as we descended the dusty stairs, I said, "She's making suckers of us."

"Perhaps there's some reason…"

On the hot pavement outside, before we parted, I said, "Celia Abdali needs to be pressed. Hard and quickly, Robbins!"

Tight-lipped, he got into his car.

25

I persuaded Emma to go with me to Rawalpindi for a night of gambling. She had once been promised a visit by Robert that hadn't materialised, but she was not enthusiastic. She was persuaded. I would enjoy being with her, but I had a much more important reason to go. I wanted to put the 'donation' money secretly in the safe deposit of Robert's friend, Carlos Remedios, who managed a branch of the Bank of Portugal in Rawalpindi. It was the only truly safe place I could think of. I didn't want to visit an Islamabad or Karachi bank openly, because I thought that banking confidentiality probably didn't go very far in Pakistan. It was likely that Robbins could find out what I was doing if he knew the name of the bank I was using. I had made the arrangement with Remedios on the telephone. He was, naturally, only too willing to oblige.

Ostensibly, though, it was to be a night out with Emma, as I was fairly sure I was being followed by Robbins' men. He would argue that this was a security measure, but I knew he was suspicious of me. I planned to get away from the casino, leaving Emma for half an hour, drop the money and return to her.

I retrieved the trunk containing the money from my obliging neighbour. I then packed the notes into a leather holdall and the pockets of my suit. I looked slightly more bulky than my usual self, but I would pass. I hired a car, which I drove myself.

I collected Emma at her apartment. As we drove, she looked at the eroded hills of the Eastern Punjab from the window of the car without interest. This turned to repulsion as the shanties, ramshackle shops and rotting buildings began to reel past.

She sighed. "Why did you want to come here, Nick? Of all places…"

"Because it's a with-it place, you'll see."

When I had parked the car at the Hotel Estoril and negotiated a fee with one of the lads roaming the lot to look after it, we checked in. Emma sniffed at the room, which was comfortable if modest. We left the hotel and emerged into a half-deserted side street with shuttered shops, and began to wade through a tide of orange peel, empty bottles, plastic wrappers and banana skins.

"God, what a smelly dump!" Emma said. "They haven't a socially conscious bone in their bodies!"

"Let's get a cab. It's more fun to ride in the open," I said.

"Why have you got that bag with you, or is that your stake?" Emma laughed.

"Could be." I wasn't letting Emma in on my plans.

We drove down the crowded main promenade in a pedicab on our way to the casino. The sky was darkening. The buildings were sapped of colour. Dirty, barefoot children were handing out cards that advertised restaurants and bars. I thought I might like to have children of my own one day, but I couldn't imagine Emma as a mother – or, when I came to consider it, a wife. She was a lover and a party ornament.

The houses we passed were decayed, their shutters askew, the balconies crumbling, and the shops were lit by feeble lamps. There was a smell of filthy drains. In the distance, on higher ground, the sun was setting on the abscesses of plastic and cardboard– the shelters of the poorest.

We were carried into an area of higher-rise buildings and more upmarket shops. We dismounted the cab and pushed through the clattering chaos of the street to enter the Paradise Club. What went on in the club was, I thought, illegal and entry was restricted to members. I was a member, but I had only visited once or twice with Robert. After the delay of going through the club's security system, we were released into ultra-luxurious spaces of ethereal artificial light. Emma was astounded. "I didn't know such places existed," she said.

After a gin and tonic, she began to expand pleasurably under the starlit dome of the main hall, with its muted background music and long, mirrored bars loaded with liquor. The green baize tables were busy and the clientele was quietly absorbed. The slot machines were segregated out of earshot in another chamber. I settled Emma at a roulette table with a fresh drink and she quickly became engrossed in the play. I left her with 500 dollars and went out to the bank, which was nearby. I didn't explain myself. Emma was the kind of self-possessed person who wasn't nervous about being alone. I hesitated, but only to make sure that I was unobserved.

Remedios was helpful and efficient and the transaction was arranged quickly. I walked briskly back to the Paradise Club, fairly sure that I had not been watched. I quickly froze out the European stranger who had seated himself beside Emma and engaged her in conversation.

When Emma turned her attention from the man to me, she said, "I'm afraid I've lost nearly all of the money you gave me, Nick." She was slightly dazed by the atmosphere and the drink.

I said it didn't matter. While the night ticked away outside, time remained stationary inside. We drifted past the tables, pausing to play where we chose. Roulette was Emma's favourite. In one game she amassed nearly 2,000 dollars and then lost it all. When I gave her more money, she shovelled chips onto the board greedily and lost them just as quickly.

I played blackjack and Emma watched until she was bored. Together, we must have lost about four thousand dollars. Emma hardly noticed. She showed no curiosity about my means. The piles of multicoloured chips excited her. A gambler in a waistcoat and shirt-sleeves threw a 200 dollar tip to one of the blackjack dealers. Long fingernails tucked the notes away in a tip cache. The roulette marbles ground ceaselessly on the wheels. Banknotes crackled. The money turned into bright chips. The chips melted from the tables. At last, I was tired.

"Let's go and get something to eat," I said, noticing for the first time that one of the people scanning the tables didn't appear to be one of the casino's security men. He was dressed in a fawn suit and I thought I'd seen him at Special Branch.

Emma didn't want to leave the tables. She was hooked. "Please, Nick, let's play a little more."

"I've just about run out of money, Emma." Actually, I had about 2000 dollars left.

"Well you shouldn't come on frolics like this if you can't afford them," she said, spitefully.

"You've had a good run, unlucky maybe. And now we'll eat."

I was firm with her. I enjoyed the casino, but I never transferred my real-life love of gambling to the green baize. I liked to be able to work out the odds for myself, rather than have to accept them blindly from a casino proprietor. We had a hamburger and a bottle of wine in the casino restaurant and went outside. It was nearly 6am on a stifling morning. I kept trying to sight the Special Branch man, but failed.

"Let's go to the other casino," Emma said, perkily. "What did you call it, the 'Rama'?"

"We'll go and have a look." I was thinking that another 1000 dollars down the drain wouldn't hurt, but I had had enough.

Emma had dark rings under her eyes. Her cheeks were flushed. I wanted to please her, but I didn't know exactly where the 'Rama' was. We hired a battered taxi rather than a pedicab. The driver seemed to know the location, but in twenty minutes took us by a circuitous route back to a different door of the Paradise Club.

I had a strained conversation, half in sign language, with the driver. He mumbled and extracted a notebook from the glove compartment. I could see an Eastern script on one page and English opposite. I leaned over and took the book, hoping to speed the process. I saw a list of girls with descriptive statistics. As I scanned the pages, the driver capped his hands over the back of the seat, allowing a vile breath to escape through his misplaced teeth.

"You want girl?"

"I want to go back to our hotel," Emma snapped.

"I'm going to walk for a while," I said. "You take the cab."

I gave the driver 10 dollars, naming the hotel, and Emma drove off in the vehicle without another word. I walked a long way past the yellow-fronted buildings while people pushed past me in the dawn light. I entered a small park on a rise that was choked with banyan trees. From this position, I was able to look across the town and see the encampment of hovels that besieged the old fortress on the rise. The air reeked of poverty and decay.

As I left the park, I saw the man I had seen in the casino slinking ahead of me. He slipped into a droop-shuttered, old stone building settling into the earth. It was a museum or an antique shop, which was, incredibly, open at this hour. Irritated, I followed. Inside, I found flaked and buckling oil paintings of nineteenth-century merchants and soldiers, dusty vases and pots, a room of faded and torn scrolls; a rusty cannon, a ship's bell and peeling religious paintings of fat white angels and madonnas.

I passed close to a screen, knowing my watcher was behind it, and spoke to him. "I saw you at the casino. Are you following me?"

"We're concerned about your safety," the man said in English and retreated, taken aback.

"Safety, my auntie," I said to his retreating back.

And then I saw the paintings, which were small, precise watercolours. Exhausted by the sight of 300 years of junk in the rooms, I now looked through twelve tiny port-holes to a new vision of Rawalpindi. The paintings portrayed the town of a 150 years ago. There, in pale yellows and blues, were old buildings comfortably asleep in the sun, soft skies and peaceful archways with flowering vines.

"Who painted them?" I asked a hovering attendant.

"A refugee… a white Russian… I believe he's dead now," he said in precise English.

"Beautiful… but unrealistic?" I said.

"I think the scenes are real. You can visit them, although they are much changed. They just don't take in all of Rawalpindi," he said, with an earnest look.

When I left the building, the Special Branch man had apparently gone. I walked back to the Estoril through the now crowded and disorderly streets, with the artist's uplifting vision in my mind.

Back in our room, I found Emma lying on the bed in her slip. She was awake. The room was cold. Her wet hair stuck to her temples. Her face glistened. I was about to ask her if she was ill, but paused at the venomous gleam in her eyes.

"Well, did you have one of those girls, Nick? Did you enjoy her?"

"The girls in the cabbie's book?"

"What others could there be?"

"Plenty, but no. I didn't have one. I walked."

"Liar!"

26

I lay beside Emma on the bed, fully dressed. She turned her back on me. My thoughts went back to our meeting at Salisbury Crown Court many years ago. After I had returned to March House that day, I recounted my experience to Robert. He listened impassively as I explained how overwrought Emma had been and how we both felt that Macbeth had suffered enough.

'She told me it wasn't Macbeth anyway, but somebody else!' I said, trying to sound threatening.

Robert was quiet for a while. He turned his eyes on me unblinkingly. I could see a shadow in the blue lake. 'You must stick to your nauseating story, Dyson, or you'll be jailed for perjury.' He spoke cautiously.

'My story is true. Hers isn't!'

'She's a hysterical fool!' Robert shouted, his features suddenly agitated.

I knew then, beyond doubt, that Robert Laidlaw was the somebody else. At that moment I hated my friend and mentor. 'It was you, wasn't it?'

Robert didn't reply directly. He gave me a wan, hopeless look and said, 'Get out of here!' in a low voice.

Emma Southern wrote a letter to Gerald Macbeth the night after our talk at the court, apologising for the pain she had caused him and saying that she knew her attacker wasn't him. She said she had been forced into the accusation by the teachers. Macbeth's lawyer obtained the letter, handed it to the judge and after a few brief enquiries, the police prosecutor decided not to proceed. The jury was discharged and Macbeth was released.

The newspapers and television channels had a hysterical day speculating on the identity of the attacker. A number of holier-than-thou persons complained that Emma should be tried for perjury. In the end, the police decided not to prosecute her. Her influential family were able to explain how distraught and confused she was after being badgered by the teachers.

With that, Emma and Macbeth disappeared from my sight for years. Emma eventually went to London for her art course and work; and although Macbeth was formally reinstated at Poole Abbey and invited to return, he never did.

I suspected that Robert was corresponding with Emma during his years in the sixth, but I had no direct evidence. On one occasion, I had the nerve to ask how Emma was. Robert had frowned and looked at me vacantly.

'Emma? Emma Southern? How the devil would I know?'

Robert was a skillful actor. He went on to become a successful head of house and seemed to give March a period of stability. When he left after his second year in the sixth, having been accepted for Cambridge, the brightness faded from the air. I was left alone with my secret.

I completed a mediocre year in the sixth and was ready to leave at the end of it. My father tried hard to find me a university place, but with my poor record, it was difficult to get into law school. A law school was my father's suggestion to which I acquiesced. When every university seemed to have been canvassed, the computerized system worked by my father offered me a place at Swansea. I embarked on a law degree which passed in a haze of casual sex and alchohol. I graduated without any distinction. My father's influence with an old school friend then got me a place in the chambers of a leading criminal lawyer in London. He overlooked my dismal degree and fell instead for the 'poor motherless boy' routine, which my father was expert in deploying.

In London, I was eventually able to take up with Emma. Winning her as a lover was beyond my most extravagant hopes. The real sparkle of London was Emma, not the dreary criminal courts.

27

When I returned from Rawalpindi with a peeved and silent Emma, she insisted on taking a taxi to her apartment. I drove the rental car to my office. I never let Emma's moods disturb me. On my pad was a message from Robbins: 'IF have been in touch. Meeting tomorrow PM. Will call in at eleven.'

It was nearly eleven now and Robbins arrived promptly.

"Have you made any more of the beautiful doctor?" I asked him as he entered.

"I've got a statement but it takes us no further. She was Laidlaw's friend, she says, rather than girlfriend, and it's simply an unhappy coincidence that whoever was tailing Laidlaw decided the best time to grab him was at the Sheraton."

"Robert could have talked to a friend in the bar or the coffee shop. Why go to room 1062 together?"

"All right. You don't expect her to admit her affair, do you?"

"What about her avoiding you? Is that consistent?"

"I think so. From the time she read what happened at the Sheraton in the newspapers she must have been worried about being dragged in. She shied away. You can hardly blame her."

"And what about her being in company with a terrorist in the hotel?"

Robbins hesitated. "We don't know how Khan fits in. I wouldn't jump to conclusions."

"I would!" I said. "It's plain that Khan was involved in Petrie's murder. By association that includes Abdali."

To me, Robbins' work looked cursory. He was less confident now than he had been at the beginning of the investigation. He appeared perturbed by lack of progress, but did little to make progress– yet I was certain that he was an intelligent and competent officer.

He had the world looking over his shoulder. Both the BBC and CNN had sent television teams to Islamabad. At least one investigative reporter from London's *Sunday Times* Insight team was in town, as well as a handful of independent journalists from the US. Up to now, all these newshounds could do was film the colourful background and get drunk at the bar of the Press Club. They were restive and all over Robbins wherever he went. The stories in the British broadsheets were getting nasty, with headlines like 'Investigation Flounders', 'Top Cop at Boat Party,' and 'Government Embarrassed by Inept Police Work.'

I drew strength from the media presence; it not only jarred Leighton and Grace into action, but shored up my position with Grace. She was, more than ever, concerned that a few stray words from me to the journalists could provoke publicity that would plunge them into an official enquiry– and her competence and reputation would be an issue. She was constrained to remain pliable and polite with me.

The angle that was missing from the media hysteria was the bleating of the Laidlaw family at home in England. Although Robert had many important political connections and was well known at Westminster, he had no immediate family other than Emma. The more remote members of his family had declined to become involved publicly. The effect was that Robert's tragedy lacked the sobbing and tears, and the agonising fleshly weakness that the media so loved to portray and exploit on camera. Emma declined to comment, mainly because Leighton had warned her that loose talk could endanger Robert. The furore around Robert's abduction was indeed more muted in Britain, but it was nevertheless fierce.

"I have a ray of light," Robbins said, coolly. "We have received information that Sir Robert has been seen on a housing estate at the end of Karnagar Road in Rawalpindi."

"How did you find out?"

"We asked the Pakistan force to approach their informers. A snitch gave a Rawalpindi station this story."

"A few dollars, and you have something."

"That's the way it works."

"Why didn't you do it sooner?"

"You're always needling, aren't you? We asked for information from the day we started the investigation."

"How are you going to play this? Are we going to have tea and buns with Leighton & Co first and think about it?"

"We've verified the genuineness of the information as far as we can. We have the area under surveillance and we've narrowed down the place where Laidlaw might be. We're ready to go in."

"It'll be a risk for Robert, bearing in mind how they dealt with Petrie." I was thinking of Robert the lover, the politician, the bon viveur, now dirty and smelly, perhaps beaten, cooped up in a concrete cell.

"No alternative. We'll cordon off the area and search the living units. The people we're seeking are fanatics. They could decide to shoot it out against the odds. Cornered, they may not give a damn. That's the way it is. And Sir Robert wouldn't get out of that."

I began to feel I was slightly more in the flow of events. I had thought I might be shut out as a result of my complaints, but the opposite had happened. I had evidently disturbed our small committee enough to make them want not only to tolerate, but to satisfy, me. I could influence Robbins, and I began to wonder how far his hesitations were caused by his bosses.

I gave him a supportive grin. "Let's do it then."

That evening, I kept my promise to Rashida Masood. I met her outside the Farouk Manaan Sun Centre and she immediately said, "Let's go somewhere in your car. I don't want the girls to see us."

I drove into the northern heights in the small Renault I had hired. At the lookout point where I parked, the mist was thick. I turned to her and she was brashly expectant. "Rashida, it's not safe to park here for any length of time."

"Just a few minutes maybe."

There wasn't much room but she didn't seem to mind. I was glad the car was too small to attempt anything more ambitious than a cuddle. For a time, I delved in her exotic softness. When we began to talk, I steered her back to Celia Abdali.

"Do you know anything about her personal life?"

Rashida shrugged, not keen to talk of another woman at this meeting. "She's said to be clever. She likes European men, they say. She's not married. You like her?"

"I've never met her. Nothing bad about her?"

"No, only gossip. She used to be a communist or something, and there was a fuss when she was appointed to the Health Commission. That's all I know— what everyone knows," she added, impatiently.

I pressed on. "Any notable boyfriends other than Robert?"

"Only young Macbeth, you know, of Macbeth Docks & Trading."

"How do you know?"

"Common knowledge. They're seen around."

It was incredible that Robert and Macbeth might be sharing a woman again. Did she lure Robert into trouble at Macbeth's wish? I was satisfied that my enquiry was done for the moment, and very well done. I gave my attention to Rashida's generous breasts which were available in her conveniently loose dress, but my mind dwelt on what she had told me. Had the raw wound between Robert and Macbeth been inflamed by another woman? And if Rashida was right that there had been issues about Celia Abdali's appointment, there would be paperwork to prove it.

I went to Robbins' office the next day to ask him about the security files. I made my initial questions sound as though I was asking out of general interest. Then, I said, "If you have a political problem with somebody, I take that it you have a file in your database."

"Absolutely." Robbins was rather proud of his own part in constructing the system database, which he then explained at length.

I waited patiently while he finished, then said, "Have you checked Abdali?"

The sudden question punctured Robbins' enthusiasm. "As a matter of fact, no. I'm sure she would be clean."

"If your system is as good as you say, you must have a file on her. She has a background of protest and radicalism. She was in trouble when she applied to join the civil service."

"I'll have a look," Robbins said, grudgingly.

"Why didn't you do it in the first place?"

"Are you suggesting I'm not giving this my best shot?"

I paused long enough to show that I was suggesting that, and Robbins stared angrily back at me. "You're not following routine procedures with important witnesses," I said.

Robbins reddened. "I've said I will make the check, but it won't make any difference! Instead of sitting on the sidelines sniping, you could be of real help by joining the raid this afternoon. It's important to have somebody who knew Sir Robert personally."

"Somebody *who knows* Sir Robert..."

Robbins was retaliating and he rode over his mistake. "I must warn you, it's dangerous."

I had a sudden fear for myself: injury, a bullet, a knife thrust, a grenade. Robbins, knew I would be alarmed.

"Any form of armed intervention here is far more dangerous than in Britain. The miscreants will be armed and undisciplined. They hold life, theirs and yours, at low value. Anyhow, I've got permission for you to come. Of course, if you don't want to..."

I don't think I showed my trepidation, partly out of pique at Robbins' attitude. I had to accept the challenge, although I thought I was a fool doing so. I should have told Robbins to do his own police work. Leighton & Co were pushing me into the mire of the investigation so that I couldn't claim I was excluded. It would then enable them to continue their own personal agendas. But if I had reneged on the earlier meeting with the IF, and if I now declined to go on the raid, it could be taken as evidence that I didn't want to be seriously involved. It might devalue any later complaint I might want to make.

"I'll do it."

28

The raid was timed for 1pm– a time when many of the residents of the warren of homes on the estate would be indoors and possibly less attentive to events happening outside.

The raiding party set off from the Special Branch building in Islamabad. We were a convoy of six small, battered saloon cars of different colours and makes, which were full of local police dressed in labourers' shirts. All weapons were hidden and would be carried into the estate in a variety of shopping bags. Robbins and I were the only Europeans, apart from his sergeant. The Pakistani police were members of an anti-terrorist group and reputedly very tough, although they looked gentle and quite harmless. The heat in the cars worried them and they appeared sleepy.

It seemed to me that if anybody had Special Branch HQ under surveillance from the road, they would guess that an operation of some kind was going to take place. I mentioned this to Robbins, but he brushed it aside.

Robbins ordered that the cars were to be parked separately in different side streets at the end of Kanagar Road in Rawalpindi. The raiders, carrying their plastic bags and baskets, converged on the estate at an easy pace. The buildings were four storeys high, lying in a number of brown concrete blocks at various angles to each other. The blocks of buildings occupied a bare area of dust with the occasional football pitch. The attempts to grow grass or nurture shrubs had failed miserably. Fifteen thousand people lived here. The background noise of people talking, playing radios, children shouting and the constant movement of feet along the external corridors at each level created a wall of sound. The only colour in the amber afternoon heat came from laundered clothing, which hung limply on poles pushed from the windows.

Robbins, Sergeant Polk and I wore straw hats with sagging brims, which made us a little less obvious in the sea of locals. We walked separately to a rendezvous on the top floor of the targeted block, on a route we had memorised from a plan. I counted the turns and flights of foul stairs against my recollection. It was difficult to imagine that Robert was could be imprisoned here, in this human anthill. Robert the free spirit. I ploughed past dozens of children and families on the stairs and through the passages, keeping my head down. I carried no weapons.

I seemed not to be noticed, but Robbins said there would be lookouts and the arrival of a European would be spotted. Illegal games would halt; dope dealers would hide their wares and sidle away to a chair and a newspaper; string beads would be drawn across the doorways of brothels and the girls would go down to the market.

"In a way, it may be helpful if we rattle them a little by our arrival," Robbins had told me earlier, "because they may try to move Sir Robert. It could give us an opportunity. I don't know. We might be lucky."

I took up a position at the end of one corridor with the reserve force. They stood around casually, hands in pockets, smoking, each one trying to look as though he was on his own. The rest of the cops had fanned out down the corridor near to the target apartment. At a signal from their corporal, they produced their weapons: Uzi automatic machine guns– small, snub-nosed death sprays. The leader hit the door and burst through it in seconds. I heard screams and two short bursts of gunfire.

The reserve squad around me abandoned their pretence and held their weapons at the ready; they crouched, watching the doorway. The effect was startlingly different from the sleepy men in the cars; now, they were hounds straining at the leash. I stepped back out of their line of sight along the passage. I shook with fear; my stomach churned. What of Robert? Hell!

The raid was over in minutes. Three men were arrested. One tried to draw a pistol as he was marched out and was cut down by a quick burst from one of the Uzis. Two prisoners, but no Robert. Robbins took me into the sparsely furnished main room. There was one other room where they thought Robert had been held. It was about 6 feet square, with the window bricked up. A pallet bed was against one wall and there was a ledge that acted as a table. The cell had a putrid smell. On the ledge were two items: an English language newspaper dated two days ago and a gas cigarette lighter with an imitation gold band.

"Deliberately left behind," Robbins said.

"I think I've seen Robert with that lighter," I said. "A good sign. He's alive and they want us to follow."

"Not necessarily. They could be playing with us. There's also this," Robbins said, pushing a large biscuit tin toward me.

I opened the lid. A stench of decay hit my nostrils. The brown-stained rag which covered a large object inside was disarranged. "What is it?"

"Don't you recognise Petrie's head?" Robbins said, with a sarcastic grimace.

"Poor bastard!"

"It shows we're on the right track, but it may lead… nowhere."

There was nothing else in the room to give a clue to how long Robert had been there, or what his condition was.

"The two men we've got may talk," Robbins said, unenthusiastically.

"It's something. Some small progress," I said, watching Sergeant Polk, ahead of me, with the box tucked under his arm.

"Maybe," Robbins said.

As our party were marching out of the estate, through the dust, I was crumbling with the anti-climax. Twenty-four hours of rising tension and then nothing except the ghoulish discovery of Petrie's head. I felt weak after this almost useless and certainly dangerous foray. I pictured a drink, a very strong gin and tonic with ice and lemon. I could almost feel a fizzing mouthful going down my throat.

As we left the grounds of the estate I looked up, attracted by shouts and a hurried flurry of people on the road ahead. About 200 yards away, men were piling into two cars. I had a glimpse of a figure with wide shoulders and a pink neck. The cars pulled out sharply, engines revving and tyres spinning up plumes of dirt.

"Fuck me!" Robbins said. "I think that was Sir Robert. There was a big man. A European, I'm sure, with fairish hair!"

He looked around in frustration, but we were too far away to do anything useful. There were too many people in the street to let off a gun and even if we had field glasses, we couldn't have read the mud-caked registration plates. Robert was alive!

"I think it was him!" I said.

166

Robbins was talking on his two-way radio. He was depressingly quiet on the drive back.

"Surely you had a team in the streets around the estate for this eventuality?" I asked him.

"We did."

"So, what happened?"

"It didn't work, did it?"

"Didn't you have motorcycles for pursuit work?"

"Yes, and it's possible one of them may have got onto the tail of the cars."

Robbins spent a few more moments on his two-way radio, before turning to me, "No luck, I'm afraid. I'll try to get something out of the two we caught."

"What a bloody screw-up," I said.

29

Celia Abdali. I reflected on how Robert captured such gorgeous females. The ID photo and the video showed that she was beautiful, with a fine-boned pale face, high cheekbones, full lips and a delicate jaw. Her eyes had a kind of intelligent charm that made you take notice.

What, I asked myself, was between Robert and Celia Abdali? Of one thing I was sure: she was not a woman to dabble with. She was a high-class woman from a wealthy family, yet the thought of Robert with a Pakistani girlfriend (or any foreign woman) was impossible. Robert was a snob. His women would have to conform to his view of the English middle-class norm. Robert would welcome and befriend a man with an Eastern wife or girlfriend, but he wouldn't have one himself. Of course, that didn't mean that he would avoid a casual and private connection.

I found myself wanting to talk to Celia Abdali for reasons that had little to do with the Laidlaw investigation. I lay in bed thinking of ways I could manipulate Robbins into enabling a meeting.

I got out of bed, shaved, showered and dressed. When I came into the hall, I could hear Ram in the other bathroom. He would have made his rounds of the apartment and satisfied himself that everything was in order much earlier. The accepted routine was that I would breakfast alone, served by Ashraf, read the papers or watch the online news, and then, when I was ready to go to the office, Ram would accompany me in the lift and as far as the chauffeured car.

This morning, the routine was slightly different. I was going to drive myself in the hired Renault so that it could be returned to the hire company. When we went downstairs and walked out of the lobby, I paused in the sun, feeling the warmth ebb into me. Ram was slightly ahead, walking toward the line of residents' cars in the shelter. I felt mildly buoyed at the prospect of the week ahead. Some firm steps would surely be taken towards finding Robert, and I sensed, for no very tangible reason, that my pursuit of Emma was advancing.

I started to move quickly, passing Ram, who observed the area as he walked. I reached the door of the car 15 feet ahead of him and had the ignition key in my hand. I opened the driver's door, tossed my briefcase onto the passenger seat and bent down to slide under the steering wheel. With a choking cry, Ram was against me, his face virtually pressed to mine. I could smell garlic on his breath in that millisecond.

"Freeze, sir! Retreat, sir!"

I was rigid, my lips almost on Ram's, looking into his terrified face. Together, we began a slow-motion move away from the car. It must have looked as though we were playing a silly game, but something was gravely, terrifyingly wrong. Ram quivered like a dog as he smothered himself around me, easing himself between the car and my body. As we slowly disengaged from the driver's door, I heard a gentle friction of metal on metal. The door swung shut. I saw fear in Ram's eyes. Then, my head exploded with a sensation that began deep inside my skull.

Grace Stewart, of all people, was sitting patiently beside my bed, reading, when I awoke. I was in my own bedroom, back in the apartment.

"I'm invading your sanctuary."

"I don't mind," I said, feeling fairly alert apart from a faint headache.

"Don't worry. You're all right. The doctor couldn't find a scratch on you. Mild concussion. He said you were just sleeping. I thought I'd sit it out until you woke. "

"Thanks. And Ram?"

"Dead, I'm afraid. He took the full force of the blast."

"He saved my life. He must have seen something as we approached the car. I should have let him check it first, but I was in a bit of a hurry. Not a real hurry, merely feeling good on a fine day."

"It looks as though you're on the hit list," she said.

"Whose? As if it matters."

"God knows, in this chaos. Robbins doesn't know."

"He doesn't know much. Robbins, I mean. I can't see why anybody would want to kill me." Even so, the image of Macbeth's cadaverous face was before me.

"The press are hyping you as the third victim in a political crime," she said, distastefully.

"Maybe it'll inject a bit of life into the hunt for Robert."

"It's difficult to do our work in an atmosphere like this. So many counter-allegations and suspicions. If anybody wanted to destabilise our efforts in Afghanistan, they could say they've done a good job. All sides are throwing stones. Some Afghans say we don't want progress, we just want to hang around as neo-colonialists. The British public obviously don't want any more servicemen sacrificed. But a responsible government can't be created overnight."

"I should think it doesn't matter if we peddle our contracts and military hardware to a corrupt government, a military junta or a democratic house of cards."

"Maybe it doesn't," Grace said, candidly, "but a lot of harm will have been done and a lot of trust lost."

I guessed she was thinking that she might not be leading the British delegation at the talks; she'd have missed her chance to distinguish herself. She'd admitted to me privately one day during lunch how lucky she was to get the appointment here. Chance retirements from the service had produced the opportunity, as well as the fact that others who were better qualified had, for some reason, had faces that didn't fit politically. A little star of opportunity had flared for her and would soon die. She would go back to being the distinguished second ranker that she was.

I had to stay in bed for a day, although I resisted it. I had a new bodyguard, Joe Nevill, who was a rookie Special Branch cop from Glasgow. Dr Van Roggen, a Dutch medical doctor who lived in the same apartment block was organised to treat me. He was employed by the High Commission.

"You'll be all right after a day's rest," he said, after taking my pulse and looking into my eyes with a torch. "You have no pain. Fine. Work tomorrow."

"Do you know Celia Abdali at the Health Commission?"

"I know of her. A very capable administrator."

"Was she a bit of a radical at one time?"

"I never heard it if she was."

"Can you tell me about her? She was the last person to see Robert Laidlaw before he disappeared."

"I don't know all that much. She seems to be a well thought of."

"Married?"

"I don't think so, but one never knows. She's certainly a career person."

When the doctor had gone, I phoned Robbins. "What progress on Abdali?"

"You were right," he said, reluctantly. "She is on file. She was a leftist activist as a student. Her US visa was withdrawn and she had to continue her studies in London."

"Agitators welcome!"

"Her appointment at the Health Commission raised objections, but they were resolved."

"She could have set Robert up."

"It's barely possible. Far-fetched. She hasn't been active in any way for years. She's been a model at the Commission. It was student radicalism, something of the past."

"What are you going to do about it?"

"Naturally, we'll keep an eye on her, but… it's pointless."

After finishing with the lukewarm Robbins, I decided to speak to Celia Abdali myself. I was interfering, but for a good cause. The tardiness of the whole High Commission group angered me. Celia Abdali took the call herself and sounded pleased, in contrast to our first encounter. She remembered me, knew exactly who I was and wasn't troubled to hide it. She'd read all about the bomb in the papers. She seemed to think that her story was now accepted and she showed no inclination to run away.

"It seems as though you're recovering all right, she said.

Her English was faultless, each word finished precisely in a BBC accent. More than the accent was her confidence. Her articulation was clearer than a native English person. We talked about the incident and there was an undercurrent of familiarity in her words. She oddly never asked the purpose of the call. When I ended it by saying, "I'd like to see you some time and talk about that last day with Robert," she simply said, "OK," and rang off abruptly.

Rashida Masood kept coming to my office on any pretext she could find, anxious to fix another clandestine meeting. I kept up her expectations, partly because she could continue to be helpful to me and, I have to admit, because I had found our previous interlude pleasurable, although not something I would have undertaken for its own sake.

I had been considering for a while how I might get access to the 'Top Secret' files. One afternoon, when Rashida was in my office flexing her body before me on a needless errand, I decided to speak to her frankly.

"Rashida, the investigation is bogged down. The big wheels don't seem to be taking an interest. I don't know what's going on, but it's not fair to Robert. I need to have a look at the Top Secret and Confidential files. Can you help me?"

Her chest swelled and her heavy eyelids drooped as she assessed the request. "You know I want to help you, Nick, but we can't talk here, can we?"

Of course we could talk in my office, but there wasn't going to be any talk unless there was a quid pro quo. "You think you could help me?"

She nodded slowly. "I think so."

"Let's meet and go for a drive on one of your bowls evenings, Rashida; it's what I've been wanting to do." I opened my eyes wide and smiled.

"Just because of the files?"

"My dear," I said, opening the palms of my hands toward her. "I'm only sitting here because not so long ago Grace Stewart barged in. If I could do what I wanted to do, I'd come around the desk, hug you and…"

She couldn't conceal an amused smile of anticipation. "All right, Nick. Enough. But bowls night is difficult. The girls, you know?"

"What do you suggest, Rashida?"

Her eyes widened. "Your place?"

"I have a security guard and a servant there 24/7. It would be embarrassing…"

"My husband is going to England in a few days to visit his mother. I think one afternoon…"

I frowned, pretending not to see. "But in the car, in the afternoon heat…"

"Not practical," she agreed.

"You mean a hotel?"

"Or maybe at my apartment."

30

The phone rang. Emma Laidlaw. It was 11pm and I had finished a piece of cold, spiced chicken Ashraf had left for me, had a quiet walk around the lawns and was preparing to read a book, rather than have a few brandies.

She was distraught. "Nick, come up here right away, will you? Please!"

"What's the matter?" I asked, alarmed.

"Something dreadful's happened. It's too horrible. I just got back from a party at the Meridian and found it," she sobbed, her voice dying away.

I tried to speak to her, but she had apparently dropped the phone. I could hear her crying. I hung up and called my neighbour to borrow his car. Nevill and I were in the lift to the garage in minutes. I drove as fast as I dared to the Langar.

When we arrived at the apartment, the door was open. I pushed it wide and walked in. The servant was by the door, frozen with shock. The hall had polished parquet tiles with white walls and bright modern prints in silver frames. The only thing out of place was that one of the prints was askew; and, now that I looked more closely, the glass on another had been shattered and the fragments were on the floor.

I had a mental picture of the lounge, the pale Tiensin rugs and white leather couches and armchairs. The effect was supposed to be minimalist. I was unprepared for what I saw when I entered. I was expecting some kind of unthinkable violence; the same kind of feeling I had had on the threshold of Petrie's execution chamber at the Sheraton. The walls, mats and curtains had been sprayed with an aerosol container of black dye. The couches had been gashed. Shattered pieces of Meissen china covered the floor; the drawers of the dresser had been pulled out and emptied, and the books raked from the bookshelves. It was chaos.

Emma was not in the desecrated room. I hurried through to the main bedroom where she was lying on the bed. This room seemed to be undefiled. Her tears had dried. Her eyes were staring.

"Somebody hates me," she whispered.

"That makes two of us." I restrained myself from saying that it could be Macbeth, but this incident seemed to me more like personal spite than a political statement. "Where's your minder and the servant?"

"He was out with me. He couldn't do anything. And it was Ranee's day off. I've called Hugh Leighton."

I found Nevill talking to Bob Locke, another young Special Branch man, in the kitchen. They were in contact with Robbins, who was going to arrange an examination of the premises and question the neighbours. It was a routine reaction. I doubted that anything would be discovered.

I encouraged Emma to have a shower and she was soon tucked up in the bed in a clinging blue-and-white, polka-dot dressing gown. The living room was too desolate to enter. I sent a reluctant Nevill back to my apartment. I mixed two martinis and told Emma about the raid, the glimpse of Robert, the bomb in my car and Celia Abdali. I let her know that Robert had been with Abdali just before he disappeared.

"The prospect of finding Robert seems to drift away and then suddenly come back," she said.

"He's alive, Emma!"

She was sorry for herself. "I was having fun here until Robert went missing; and then that funny thing with the speedboat and now this. Even if Robert comes back safe, he'll never be able to carry on. The government will replace him after all the rumours and gossip and speculation about his private life. Those people at the High Commission have quietly ruined him. They're jealous of him. And we'll have to go back to England where Robert doesn't have a career or even a seat in parliament."

I was drawn to her, in spite of her shallowness. The feeling I had for her seemed to be all the sharper because she was so selfish and because she wasn't capable of being possessed. It was perverse of me, but that's the way I felt.

"Come back to England with me, Emma." It was becoming a mantra.

She ignored me. "We both seem to be targets for somebody. Do you think somebody wants to kill me or frighten me?"

"I honestly don't know; it could be political. Robbins thinks we could both be targets– or it could be Macbeth."

"Oh, Nick, you're like a paranoid old granny, casting suspicions without a sensible cause. I'm sure you're wrong about Gerry. I think he's glad to make up after all these years. After all, he is a civilised man. He wouldn't resort to violence, to bombs, to trashing apartments."

"Emma, there are some events that happen between people that are so grave that they can never have a future together, whether as friends or lovers or spouses. They simply have to part."

Emma's apparent ignorance– or it may have been

denial– of the depth of the hurt she had done to Macbeth, continued to baffle me. I believed there was no way Emma and I could make up for the false accusation of Macbeth, his expulsion in disgrace, the ordeal of a prison sentence dangling like a noose over his head for months.

I believed Emma's contrition, but the withdrawal of the prosecution and the invitation to Macbeth to return to Poole Abbey could never make up for his suffering. It may have made some difference that Macbeth's family, living in Pakistan, were at such a distance from these events, but the personal impact on the man was written on his face even today. Macbeth had completed his education in the USA, presumably insulated from the past, but could one ever forget it?

I never gave up trying to convince Emma that of all the men on the planet, Macbeth was the one to be avoided. She saw the world as she wanted it to be. I think she even supposed that she and Macbeth could continue as lovers – perhaps, in her most wayward dreams, as husband and wife! These were painful thoughts for me.

I stayed at the Laidlaw apartment that night. The turmoil of my relationship with Emma seemed to heighten the passion I indulged on her in bed. It was like a drug I couldn't give up. But in the morning, with Emma beside me, naked and sleeping lightly, my thoughts moved back to Celia Abdali and the question of her involvement in Robert's disappearance.

After the news of the trashing of Emma's apartment had been received with due seriousness, Robbins was upbeat at the meeting held at the High Commission that morning to report on the progress of the investigation. The raid, the arrest of suspects, the sighting of Robert and the surveillance of Celia Abdali were all positive events, and they tended to show that he was, at least, advancing. I was probably the only one present who was aware of the extent of Robbins's uncertainties and the malaise that seemed to mire him.

When Robbins had finished, I said, "I'm concerned that we don't seem to be discussing all the relevant information about Robert at this meeting."

"We can't review every activity here," Hall retorted, savagely.

"No, but points that ought to have been mentioned, haven't been."

"What do you mean, ought to be? Are you the arbiter?" Hall snapped.

"It was intolerable and embarrassing to learn in a meeting with the business lobby that complaints have been made to you about Robert taking bribes."

"Discretion, Mr Dyson. Complaints are two a penny until we have evidence," Hall responded, with his arid smile.

"Absolutely," Leighton echoed, sardonically. "Laidlaw's good name is everything."

"This meeting was entitled to know that a complaint had been made, regardless of whether you had evidence. Robert's good name is not going to suffer in this confidential meeting. Now, what evidence do you have, Leonard?"

"I'm not prepared to talk about it– it's a matter under investigation."

"Facts about who made the complaints and the nature of them, could provide clues in Robert's investigation," I insisted.

Hall looked around at Leighton for support but he maintained a taut silence. Leighton– and Grace– seemed apprehensive of an open complaint of dissatisfaction from me. They listened but said little.

We could hear the chink of cutlery and plates on the veranda as the maid laid the table for lunch. Robbins said that there had been no further sighting of Robert, in an attempt to move away from my line of enquiry.

"What about the two men you arrested in the raid?" I asked. "They seem to have been forgotten."

"We'll have to see about them," Robbins said, vaguely.

I couldn't understand Robbins's virtual lack of interest in the men. I gave up that line of questioning, too. I handed round a file of press clippings, which showed that the news media believed the investigation was going nowhere. "When you see these, you may understand why I'm saying we should have more manpower to help Dennis and a clear action plan. We don't even have minutes of these meetings."

I had, however, begun to take minutes myself, rather ostentatiously, and this was an irritant to the others. They passed the file of clippings from one to another without more than a glance at them.

"Action plans?" Hall said. "This isn't a business development exercise. It's a police investigation. All avenues have been followed in a timely way."

"Not in my opinion. The Abdali involvement would never have been uncovered if I hadn't become concerned."

Hall responded with a hack of laughter. "Our amateur detective! Abdali leads nowhere– a waste of time!"

"Are we going to get any report about the views of the Pakistan Government and the FO on an exchange of prisoners?"

"There's nothing to report," Grace said. "Naturally, I've told the FO about the request to exchange."

"You haven't explored the possibility of an exchange?" I said, my voice shrill with suppressed pique. "Robert's an important person. Something could be worked out with the Pakistan authorities."

"I don't think so," Grace said, heavily.

"Even if it didn't come off, it would give us more time," I persisted.

Leighton glowered at me. His natural instinct was to humble a recalcitrant junior, or even dismiss him from future meetings. But he couldn't quite assess how much of a menace I was. An unproven allegation that Robert had been taking bribes made no difference to the need for strenuous efforts to save him. I thought that Leighton was swiftly exploring in his mind whether he should have asked London to consider an exchange.

Bradshaw said, "You know my opinion on this, Grace. I wrote you a note. I think HMG can twiddle a couple of knobs in the Pakistan Government. There are precedents. We've done it with the Saudis. The US did it with Iran. Robert's a special case as the main representative of our government. The point is that we wouldn't be responding to threats. It would be a unilateral act by the Pakistan Government."

It seemed to me that Bradshaw might be thinking ahead to an official enquiry and, in putting his views in writing, had taken out an insurance policy for himself. Leighton was staring at him very seriously and was certainly making a similar calculation.

"Perhaps we need to consider this further," he said. "Let's meet tomorrow and decide how to tackle it. Agreed?"

He was reserving the opportunity to make the grand plea to the FO for himself, which Grace should have made.

Poor Grace had to agree, unless she insisted she was going back to her office to compose an email that contradicted what she had just said to us. Leighton stood up and declared the meeting closed, nodding approval at a maid who was carrying an armful of blossoms through to the veranda to decorate the lunch table.

"You're leaving it a bit late," I said, but felt pleased.

Later that day I went to the Special Branch office to meet Robbins and to see the information that had been obtained from the interrogation of the two arrested men.

"It's not much," Robbins said grimly, casting the papers on the desk.

I picked up the English translation of the statements of the two men and was amazed at the detail. They admitted abducting Laidlaw from the Sheraton and killing Pirie, they also named their accomplices, although each statement named different people.

I looked questioningly at Robbins. "Not much? I don't know what you mean. This is really important."

Robbins put his head on one side and squinted at me.

"You mean the confessions are false?" I said.

"The result of over-keen police work, I'd say. These two would confess to breaking and entering Buckingham Palace if you wanted them to."

31

My wristwatch read 8.30pm. I was virtually alone inside the High Commission building except for the security guards and the odd cleaner. I entered the safe on the third floor, which Rashida had told me contained the archive of hard-copy Top Secret files. The lighting was feeble, but enough. I was disappointed to find that the files had expired five years earlier– and I assumed that all the subsequent material was held online. I thought, however, that these old files might contain information about Abdali's earlier activities. I was confronted by a massive array of paper and an almost incomprehensible index system.

The combination of the safe was the only information I had been able to get from Rashida Masood after an afternoon spent with her urgent honey body at the Hilton Hotel. At the time, I thought it was enough. Now, I wasn't sure whether she was doling out the information slowly to found our relationship more firmly, or simply doing her best.

After half an hour of poring over the index, I was able to locate two files that referred to Abdali. Instead of reports about her conduct, they were reports by her, to Leonard Hall, about figures in the Pakistan Government. I was astounded. I skimmed them quickly. I doubted that the reports were very important now, but she was undeniably an informer. I closed the safe and came away from the building realising that if Leonard Hall knew Abdali was an informer, Robbins must also have heard of her. But Robbins had tried to paint her as an innocent civil servant who was accidentally implicated as a lover. It seemed to me that it could only be that he was trying to protect her.

But there was more to come from Rashida. She thought she could get Grace Stewart's entry code into the computer system. I'm good with computers, but I'm not a hacker.

Rashida said she had heard Grace admit to the technical officer responsible for computer security that she would have to make a note of the password, which was admittedly complicated, in her pocket book. On more than one occasion, Grace had sought Rashida's help in entering the password. Rashida was regarded in the office as computer-savvy. Elaborate security and entry criteria had been concocted, without much thought of how a user could call them to mind on the infrequent occasions of use. This might be a prize for me on another day.

I had begun to sleep fitfully. Nevill, the officious guard, didn't help. Anxious to do a thorough job, he prowled the apartment at night, disturbing me. I would wake at a sound in the middle of the night after a lurid dream about the Sheraton charnel house, or Robert and I at Poole Abbey where an infinitesimal grievance had been expanded in my imagination to something life-threatening. I sat up in the moonlight listening to the clacking of insects when the air-conditioner was off.

In the night, strange ideas came with a clarity that seemed to testify to their credibility. It was possible that Robert was the victim of Macbeth. Macbeth was well able to engage hitmen who were untraceable and to have discreet connections with terrorists. Macbeth, himself, was an Urdu speaker. He was a near as you could get to a white native. In the 1830s, Karachi had been a village at the mouth of the Indus, used as an occasional refuge by pirates and a repair place for battered trading ships with its deep and sheltered water. Macbeth's ancestors, who were British traders and seamen, arrived. One could call them pirates. In the ensuing 250 years, they prospered with Macbeth Docks and Trading, which was now quoted on the stock exchanges of London, New York and Tokyo. The company, Macbeth and his family, were indissolubly linked with the East. He could command forces that Westerners could barely understand. He looked like a businessman from the City of London and spoke like one, but in reality he was part of an alien and, to me, obscure Eastern world.

The man haunted my dreams. He drove the shadows of sleep away with the darker shadow of his presence. I had known before I came to Pakistan that the old enmity with Macbeth would not die; and my experience here had taken me further. I had the intuition that Macbeth intended to kill me and Emma. He had already dealt a blow to Robert by traducing him, and perhaps even facilitating his capture by terrorists. And what part had Macbeth and his girlfriend, Celia Abdali, played on the day of Pirie's death in luring Robert into danger? I had given myself a headache trying to fathom why Robert, in his desperate plight, should communicate the one word, 'Macbeth', unless it was to point to the man who had placed him in mortal danger.

What fools we had been to come here! The car bomb and the wrecking of Emma's apartment weren't imaginary, but viewing them as an act of political vindictiveness by a group of anti-British terrorists seemed a feeble hypothesis; they were menacing actions of a very personal kind.

Would Macbeth have sacrificed Petrie, the security man,

to get at Robert? If Macbeth was going to engineer the abduction of Robert by terrorists, leading in all likelihood to Robert's death, Petrie was merely a pawn. I feared Macbeth could strike again at any time and in ways we could never anticipate.

I was in Macbeth's territory and so was Emma. I had to get out and take her with me.

I subsided at last into a disturbed sleep.

The day before I was due to fly to Kabul with Grace for a meeting, she told me that I was not on the team. She came into my office, refused a seat and made the announcement quite matter-of-factly. When I asked why, she said it was her decision. She made it apparent that she had cleared it with London (no doubt with hints of my 'unreliability'). It was a disappointment, but only a mild one, because I was preoccupied with finding Robert and getting out of Pakistan. Going to Kabul, however interesting, was a distraction. I simply shrugged and remained silent. Grace had been expecting a row, and after a moment's silence, she moved to the door, saying over her shoulder, "I thought I should tell you personally, Nick, that's all."

"I'll have plenty to occupy me in keeping this tardy investigation going," I replied.

She turned back and drew a breath to speak, but instead bit her lip and walked out.

I was still glad of this development when Robbins came into my office in the afternoon.

"Interesting news," he said, settling himself in a chair, apparently chewing it over for a few seconds. "We have a message from the IF that they're going to execute Robert at midnight on Saturday, unless we've made firm arrangements to handover the two prisoners they want."

"But there won't be time… How far have you got with it?"

"Hugh Leighton is talking to London."

"Shit! Talking to London? How long is this bureaucratic wanking going to go on! A man's life is at risk!"

"These things take time," Robbins said, mildly.

"We must get a message straight back to the IF, saying the release is being arranged and asking for the time to be extended."

"I doubt if they'll extend. They probably don't seriously expect the demand to be met. And I can't be sure our contact can get that request through."

"You're always negative. Let's bloody well try!"

Robbins didn't agree. He said, "I think we've located Robert."

I was so startled to hear this that I didn't press the point. "Why didn't you say this straight out when you came into the room? So, what are we going to do?"

"Have a go at a rescue before midnight on Saturday."

"Where is he?"

"We think he's being held on a boat at a place called Sabowal, a remote inlet on the Indus quite a way from here. Hordes of fishermen and boat people live there. It's a good place to hide and difficult to attack because all of the craft are moored together in a cluster and the river is swollen and treacherous."

"How did you get this tip?"

"Various sources."

"Don't give me sources. Getting information from you is like trying to squeeze juice from a dried walnut."

"We've traced associates of the two men we picked up on the Chunagar Estate. We've got men up at Sabowal and we're trying to pinpoint the exact boat. I'll tell you when we've got firm information and we can make a plan of attack."

"You haven't told me about the report on the bomb under my car."

"I thought you might ask that," Robbins said, taking an envelope from his breast pocket and extracting a piece of paper. "Take a look."

I scanned the paper, a brief forensic report. I was looking for something that, however remotely, might connect it with Macbeth, but that was a foolish hope. I was surprised to see that the bomb had been detonated by an electric impulse sent by an observer and not by a trip mechanism. I felt the sweat prickle under my arms as I read. The bomb parts and plastic explosive had originated in Europe.

"What's your conclusion?" I asked.

"It's not much help."

"Terrorists don't usually hang about the scene waiting to press the button."

"True, but that doesn't get us anywhere."

"It's not the material used by local terrorists and Al Qaeda, is it?" I said, taking a guess.

"No, but that doesn't mean that it wasn't placed by terrorists. If not terrorists, then who?" Robbins asked. "Do you have somebody in mind?" he added, sarcastically.

"Macbeth! Macbeth, Abdali, Robert, the Sheraton Hotel rendezvous– there's your connection."

"Oh," Robbins groaned, "don't let's go into that!"

32

I attended a brief meeting with Grace Stewart and Bradshaw when they returned from Kabul. Grace was as bland as usual, but I could tell from the heaviness under her eyes and her stiffness that all had not gone well. Bradshaw told me before the meeting that they had arrived in Kabul tired from their flight and were taken by car to the British Embassy. Storms swept clouds of dust through the streets and squares, seeping into every crack in their skin and in their hair. He was cutting about the standard of the accomodation. "Like a university hall of residence! Ugh!" An email had been waiting for Grace from the FO in London when she had arrived, saying the Ambassador to Afghanistan would head the talks. It was a blow.

"We're making the usual muck of it?" I said.

Grace was so irate beneath her calm that she seemed willing to talk freely. "Office politics. Engineered, I regret to suspect, by Hugh Leighton. He couldn't get the role himself and managed to queer my pitch. Don't ask me how."

"Friends," Bradshaw said.

"He's been put out by Laidlaw's appointment and then mine. I can't really blame him," Grace said.

"The talks are a poisoned chalice anyway," Bradshaw said.

"Bound to fail?" I asked.

"Bound not to reconcile the irreconcilable: Afghanistan and democracy," he replied.

"How about the infrastructure contracts for water and electric power and security contracts for muscular ex-soldiers?"

"Some progress there," Grace said.

"So all was not lost," I said.

"Not at all, dear boy," Bradshaw said. "Our virginity is still intact."

"Sounds like a phoney mission to me," I said.

"It isn't actually phoney," Grace said.

"Is phoney the right word for twiddle-diddling with democratic ideas while copping nice contracts?" Bradshaw whispered.

Grace looked squarely at me. "I do what I'm required to do. I don't go around putting tags on my government's policies."

I went back to my office trying to fit Robert into this picture. I could see that it might be convenient not to find him. His appointment at the time must have seemed ideal, but in post he had shown himself resistant to the wisdom of the FO and very much a salesman for British industry. He had sung the praises of democracy publicly, but believed it was not something that could be bestowed by the British and the Americans. A bad smell of bribery was gathering around his name and, although public support to find him could not be lessened, the most convenient thing would be if he disappeared completely. That was a euphemistic way of saying it would be most convenient if he was executed by the terrorists.

33

It was New Years Eve and I was tired and depressed. I had already consumed two vodka martinis when I called at Emma's apartment for a drink and found her dressed for a party. The apartment had been renovated in the few days after it was trashed and this had had a reassuring effect on her.

She was prancing around the lounge and admiring herself in the mirrors. "I may not be that long at Geoffrey's place," she said, offhandedly.

We were supposed to be going to Bradshaw's party, which would be free of aged senior diplomats. It would be buzzy.

"Why?"

"I've been asked to Gerry's party."

I had heard of Macbeth's party. All the cosmopolitan great and good of Islamabad would be there. "You're not serious."

"Of course!"

"You're coming back to my place afterwards, aren't you?" I asked, very disappointed.

"Mmmm, yes, but I may be late at Gerry's."

"You're inviting trouble."

She whirled around in her black-and-blue, satin, off-the-shoulder dress. "I'm not going to miss the party of the year."

"You're tempting fate," I said, loudly.

"I've thought it over, Nick, and those things that

happened on the boat and here couldn't conceivably be put down to Gerry. Why don't you come?"

"I can't gatecrash a party like this."

"Yes, you're right. Everybody there will be… known, not anonymous…"

"Anonymous what?"

"I was going to say civil servants," she said, impishly.

"That's what I am, is it? An anonymous civil servant?"

"Isn't that what you are, Nick, really?"

It was extraordinary that I could allow this humiliation from her. She went to her bedroom to finish her preparations. When she returned to the lounge ten minutes later, I had consumed yet another martini. She looked radiant. To my surprise, she paused, looking at me across the room.

"Oh, you do look good, Nick. The dinner jacket suits you." She smoothed her hands over the lapels and kissed me lightly on the lips. "Don't take what I said before to heart, but we do have to face simple facts. It doesn't mean I don't care for you, and it doesn't mean that you aren't a marvellous lover."

"It just means I'm a dull, little pencil pusher."

"Never dull," she laughed. "Just poor. Well, apart from that 100,000 bucks you've snugged away. Our little secret. Not that a hundred thousand would last long anyway. Unless it was more than that. I thought it was more at the time." She raised her eyebrows, hopefully.

"I'm afraid not. I've thought about it and the money will go to the party in London."

She was fascinated– no, obsessed– by Macbeth and his wealth and power, this man she had nearly destroyed. I couldn't reply. I stared at her.

Suddenly, her face reddened and she said petulantly, "All right! I won't go. You've spoiled it for me with all your grim surmises!"

We drove to Bradshaw's. He had a large apartment in a block near mine. Tonight, it was filled with his many young acquaintances from the diplomatic and business communities. I lost Emma as soon as we entered. She flitted away in the direction of a smile or a whisper. I went on, bored by trivial and inane conversations for at least two hours. For protection, I kept up with my drinks. Then, I set out to find her. I couldn't see her anywhere. I hunted Bradshaw down and asked him if he'd seen her.

"Went about half an hour ago, old boy. To Macbeth's. The biggest bunfight in town tonight."

I should have realised. Two glasses of champagne and she would see everything differently. I had my driver standing by downstairs. I had had enough liquor to dare to tell him to take me to Macbeth's home in Jinnah Drive. I was banking, somewhere deep in my mind, on the belief that Macbeth would never make his real feelings public. Therefore, even if I was discovered in his house uninvited, there would be little fuss. I did not realise that in the light of sobriety this was a questionable piece of reasoning.

The house was outside the city, situated on an elevated promontory of parkland with wide views. I intended to decide finally whether I would go in when I got there. All my experience of big receptions and parties told me that invitations are rarely produced or inspected. There would be plenty of opportunity to slip in with the crowd. It was after 11pm and many of the guests were still arriving, some of them as inebriated as I was.

At the gate, where I dismissed my driver, there was a queue of cars and a security guard with a list. I gave Bradshaw's name, knowing it would be an hour or more before he got rid of the guests at his own party. At the main door of the house, a young woman was collecting invitation cards, but clearly not everybody had brought one. While she was engrossed with guests, I slipped around her and into the throng. One simply had to have the nerve.

I took a glass of champagne from a waiter's tray and decided to have a look at the house, calculating that in the crowd, I could keep out of the way of my host.

This house, designed by the younger Saarinen, was regarded with awe in Islamabad for its expensive modernity. There were three lounges with terraces leading off from a central hall in three directions, all with superb views. I could dodge around between these as I chose. I guessed there were at least 150 guests present. I saw Emma dancing in one of the rooms, but I wanted to leave her to herself for a while. She wouldn't go home until she'd tasted the place.

I helped myself to more champagne and found a space on a bench in the well-lit garden where there was a slight breeze. Through the windows, I caught a glimpse of a tall and elegant Pakistani woman, long-necked, her hair piled high. It was Celia Abdali. I was beginning to think I could see this party out for quite a while as I helped myself to a pastry from the tray of a passing servant. Perhaps I had lapsed into paranoia completely about Macbeth. I toyed with the thought.

"Mr Bradshaw?"

The question was addressed by an attendant, a muscular Japanese man in a dark suit with a face like a moon. I knew that the visit was over.

"My name's Dyson," I said, looking past the man dismissively.

He stood squarely in front of me. "Come with me, sir," he said with authority. With one big hand under my armpit, he lifted me to my feet. He propelled me forward up the garden steps, down a hall, to a library. Gerald Macbeth was waiting. He stood in front of the bookcases, one hand in his trouser pocket, relaxed. He stared at me expressionlessly, brooding.

"I came to get Emma Laidlaw and take her home," I said, before he could speak.

He ignored what I said and sat down at the desk, spreading his hands, palms down, under a lamp. He spoke in a low voice without looking at me. "Emma Southern, Laidlaw and you, Dyson. I never thought I'd ever see any of you again in my lifetime and now you're all here in Islamabad– and you, Dyson, are trespassing in my house. Is there any limit to your impudence and conceit?"

"I did what I had to do years ago and I told the truth."

"The whole proceeding was a lie, Dyson. You told the school and the police and you were prepared to stand up in court."

"I told the truth about what I saw."

"Many times I've murdered you in my heart, so I won't waste any more time with you." He turned to the Japanese attendant. "Take him away. March him through the house, down the drive and kick him out of the gate. Let everybody see the spectacle!"

I was bundled roughly out of the door. I could hear Macbeth's hard laughter, though it seemed forced. Although I was concerned about looking a fool, my mind, soaked in alchohol, still noted that the momentary satisfaction Macbeth got from this meeting was in no way balanced by the suffering he had endured at Poole Abbey. The guard pushed and prodded me through the crowd, grasping me by the collar and one arm. I kept my eyes down, but I couldn't help noticing the surprised faces that were turned in my direction. He dragged me down the drive. At the gate, he kicked my arse very hard. I fell in the road. I climbed sorely into a cab with help from a waiting taxi driver, while the bouncer nodded and pointed and laughed.

On the way back in the cab, the effect of the drink and the public humiliation I had suffered led me into a trance. I agonised whether Emma had seen me, or anybody else who knew me. I didn't notice that the driver missed a crucial turn that would have taken us into Islamabad central. When I started to pay attention, we were flying past the decrepit shacks in the outskirts of Rawalpindi. I started to shout at the driver, but he took no notice, except to grin. He seemed to know his destination. A few moments later, he drove the car off the road and stopped in a compound fringed by decrepit buildings. I was scared. I jumped out.

There was light from one feeble lamp and the moon, but otherwise I seemed to be in a dark wasteland. The cabbie didn't wait for the fare. He drove off in a flurry of dust, having made his delivery. I knew I had been conveyed to a place for punishment or worse.

This could have been a set-up for a robbery, but I had very little money on me. It had to be more than that– worse than that. There were dark figures a few yards away. They didn't approach me. They had a box with a dog in it. It wasn't a robbery; they were going to set the dog on me. The animal was no more than about 15 inches high with broad shoulders, a squat head, wrinkled face and protruding jaws. I thought it was a pit bull. I have always been uneasy with dogs and I had read that this breed never let go once they get a hold. I felt sick and terrified.

This could only be retribution designed by Macbeth, who would have had plenty of time to set it up from the moment I was found in the house. I should have realised that every room contained CCTV. He must have been watching. It was clear to me that the dog handlers were waiting with their animal for my arrival.

The two men never emerged from the dark, but released the animal from its box. One man jabbered commands and pointed to me and I stemmed the dog's first rush with my foot. I scooped up two handfuls of dust and stones from the ground. I threw the contents in the eyes of the dog as it made its second charge. It yelped and fell back. Then it came again, leaping high as I sidestepped. The animal caught the sleeve of my jacket, but I swung around until the material of my sleeve was torn away and the brute rolled in the dust. I kicked it in the face. The dog shook its head stupidly and lunged at me again with breathless high-pitched barks.

The charges were becoming more effective each time. Eventually, the dog would get a hold on my leg or arm that I couldn't break. My only hope was to put a fence between me and the dog. The dog's attacks had backed me over to the side of a building. I eased along it, keeping the dog at bay with a furious onslaught of kicks.

There was a wooden fence behind the building which was about 5 feet tall. When I thought that I had enough space between me and the dog, I turned my back and took the three or four paces to the fence, springing at it. However, the dog was too quick and clamped its jaws on my ankle from behind. I fell back on the ground. I bent down and poked my fingers into the dog's eyes, drove them deep, with a strength powered by the agony of the dog's jaws on my ankle. There was no let-up. The dog only clamped harder and shook its head. My leg was red hot with pain.

I felt the earth for a stone, for anything. My fingers closed round what seemed to be a broken tile. I used it as a bludgen, hammering the beast's head and pushing the most pointed edge into its eye sockets. I struggled with the dog until it suddenly released its grip and went limp. My human attackers were still standing in the dark, well back, watching. I clawed myself over the fence and dragged myself away.

I must have hidden among deserted sheds for half an hour before I limped to the road and started to walk in what I thought was the direction of Islamabad. I was completely lost and disorientated. I moved painfully slowly, not daring to look at my damaged leg. After half an hour or so, I saw a cab stop at a streetlight. The passenger was out of the vehicle, paying off the driver. Before the driver could pull away, I slipped into the back seat and waved a few dollar bills in his face. Only when I was on my way did my fear subside and the full extent of the pain hit me.

When I got to the apartment, I found that Emma had not arrived. It was 3am. Ashraf was awake. I showed him the wound and, without comment, as though it was quite natural to deal with this, he fetched hot water, bathed the wound and produced a pungent grey ointment that he applied to the teeth marks. I decided to call a doctor in the morning.

I sent Ashraf to bed and tossed my ruined dinner suit into the rubbish bin. I lay down on the couch in the lounge in my dressing gown, my leg throbbing. After a while, I saw the lights of a car climbing the cut in the hill that led to the apartment block. I hobbled out onto the terrace. The car stopped underneath. It was a Bentley limousine. Emma slid out and went into the ground-floor foyer. When she arrived at the door, I was waiting for her.

"Hullo," she said, cheerfully. "Had a wonderful time. I'm just about wacked."

"Like a nightcap?"

"Not me. Can't you sleep, Nick?"

I was worried that she may have witnessed or at least heard of my ignominy, but it was the first thing she would have mentioned. No, I had been tossed aside like the anonymous civil servant I was. Nobody noticed. "I thought I'd wait up for you. I've got a sore leg. A dog bit me."

"I noticed you're limping. I thought that you must have gout. How strange, on New Year's Eve. Bitten by a dog. Did you stray into somebody's backyard? You must have been drunk."

"A little, I suppose. I've been thinking, there's only a few hours for us to save Robert."

Emma's expression darkened. "Oh, that. We can't do anything about it now. Let's go to bed and think about it tomorrow."

34

Two days later, my leg was much improved. I arrived at my office at 5.30am to give myself at least a few hours before anybody else came in. I strolled across the garden in front of the offices. The air was damp and hushed. The water in the fountain spattered weakly, dribbling from the upturned mouth of a slimy, green, stone fish. Splashes of red hibiscus blossomed against the hedges. I entered the portico and went past the security men with a nod, then up the stairs to my office.

I powered the computer and entered the password which Rashida had given me. It worked and I was in the Top Secret library. This was the present from Rashida, after an afternoon spent with her at her home and in her marriage bed. I was agnostic, but I couldn't help remembering that the bed had been dominated by a figure of Christ on the cross fixed above the bedhead. Rashida was a devout Catholic, I gathered, but in no way bothered by our frolicking in such a place.

I wasn't concerned that in a few days or even hours, Grace would learn from the log that somebody had used her code to enter the system.

As it was when I penetrated the safe earlier, I was confronted by a mass of enigmatically indexed data with little idea how to pinpoint the information I wanted. The files, I found, were mostly comments between London and Islamabad on high-level policy, political issues, with vignettes of local politicians and their views. All of this was of no interest to me. There were intelligence reports from agents in Iraq, India and Afghanistan, and studies of interrogations– the kind that Robbins was an expert in conducting. All of this, again, was of no apparent interest.

I found an index of personal names. I recognised names that Robbins had used in connection with information about the IF. I also found a page headed 'Celia Abdali'. It contained brief notes of reports by her. There was a recent report on the disappearance of two consultants, or security agents, one American and one British, in Afghanistan. Abdali had met the pair in Islamabad before their disappearance and had reported on their mission. Meetings and telephone conversations with Robbins, Robert, Hall and various members of the business lobby, including Macbeth, were recorded. I read quickly to get a flavour.

Abdali seemed to be in contact with some extreme groups (not specifically IF, as far as I could see) and a number of powerful lobbies, obtaining and passing information to Special Branch. There was actually no reason why a woman like Abdali, a respected senior civil servant, would act as an informer to Special Branch. It did not sit well with her former student radicalism. Even a complete change of heart would not explain it. I could only conclude that she must be a double agent, a go-between, useful to Pakistan and Britain. I had no time to ponder about her strange psychology and what she might get out of the role, apart from money.

I read the notes relating to Macbeth and Robert carefully. Macbeth's assertion that Robert was taking bribes was recorded. Robert had talked to Abdali about the various companies competing for contracts, admitting his acquaintanceship with some of the people named by

Macbeth as offering bribes. I felt sorry for Robert – he hadn't known that he was bedding a spy and a sophisticated one, who could get him to talk. Robert's favourite subject was himself and he loved to dilate upon it.

Macbeth complained that his company was prejudiced by Robert's improper activities and that Robert ought to be removed. He had also made direct representations in London. Hall was investigating the allegation and Leighton (the snake!) had communicated it to the FO. What pleasure this must have given him!

What became clear to me, as I read further, was that Robbins knew a great deal more than he had ever revealed at our steering group meetings and that Abdali was a source he had been trying to protect.

I was sitting back in my chair, surprised and confused, when there was a brisk knock and Grace entered. The time had passed quickly. It was 8.30am.

"I've piled all the current files on your desk, each with an explanatory memo," I said, to hold her off.

"Fine. Thanks."

Grace moved closer and saw the screen before I could cut the power. She realized that something was wrong.

"Are you looking at my files?"

I thought there was no point in trying to evade her. "Yes, and I find a sorry story."

"How did you do this, Nick?"

"I'm an expert hacker and isn't it a little beside the point? I now know what you've been doing."

"What do you mean?"

"Trying to get rid of Robert on the basis of unsubstantiated allegations by Macbeth."

"Not so unsubstantiated. There have been a number of complaints. Hugh Leighton was dealing with them."

"Robbins told me that Abdali was being watched from the time she was found to be involved. I was the one who involved her, not him. And all the time, Robbins was in touch with her as a police informer! Hall told our meeting that Abdali led nowhere. She's been at the heart of this whole rotten business. You knew that, didn't you?"

Grace was silent for a moment. She gestured feebly. "The police have their methods. You had no right to look at my files. It's secret information. You could be prosecuted for what you've done."

"I listened to Robbins and Hall telling lies, which you were well aware of, in a meeting set up to find Robert. You don't seem to understand. It's evident that the timing and direction of the search for Robert have been much more in the hands of Robbins and Hall than they have stated. And the reason for that seems to be a parallel and secret investigation into whether Robert was taking bribes."

"It's certainly a legitimate subject of enquiry," Grace said.

"Not if surmises and unproven allegations inhibit the search. A man's life is at stake!"

"I don't think that's happened."

"Well, I have a note of the meetings– and the lies. You don't want to find Robert because you're worried about disgracing the British Government. And let's not forget that you have a personal interest in getting your post confirmed. You don't quite know what to do and prevarication, one of the most useful tools in the kit of the civil servant, is all you can manage."

Grace floundered. "Certainly, there could be serious disgrace if…"

"You're completely misguided. What you don't know is that Gerald Macbeth and Robert have a history that goes back 20 years. They are enemies. Macbeth would do anything to smear and drag Robert down. Allegations by Macbeth are worthless."

"I know nothing about that."

"That's right. Neither you or Leighton know anything about what could be behind the bribery allegations, because you've conspired at our meetings to keep quiet about them. If you lot had been open about what you knew, I would have told you what I know. But you've used the allegations to your advantage and to Robert's prejudice. That is unfair and dangerous for Robert."

Grace could see how volatile the situation was. She was too smart to rebuke me any further for accessing the secret files. She stepped toward the door and then returned. She came around the desk and put her hand on my shoulder.

"Nick, the search for Robert is going to go on. There's no reason for you to lose faith in it or to become agitated."

"You never stop thinking about protecting your back, do you? You don't want me to complain and call for an enquiry into how you and Leighton and your lying intelligence officers have bungled the investigation."

"That's ridiculous!"

"You've had a go-slow on finding Robert. You've been anticipating that if he's found at all, he'll be dead."

Celia Abdali had seemed relaxed when I had suggested that we meet and it gave me some misty ideas that I might advance the investigation by seeing her. I realised, when I read the Top Secret files, that I had been more than a little influenced by the fact that she was a mysterious and beautiful woman. I wasn't thinking straight. Now I knew the truth about her, that she was a viper and a double-dealer who had led Robert into a trap, I loathed her. Her warped psychology was certainly interesting, though, and I had an aggressive wish to dismantle it under questioning. I decided I would try to see her. It didn't matter to me that she would probably report to Hall.

When I called her, she accepted a date at the Marriott Hotel Coffee Shop with alacrity. I was early and occupied a table so that I could watch the entrance. She arrived five minutes late, sweeping in regally with a smile. She was dressed in the Western style, as she had been at the Sheraton, but this time in a dark blue suit with a white ruffle at her throat, her long hair flowing freely and dark glasses. She steered determinedly towards me through the tables, many of which were occupied. She had no hesitation in selecting me as her host.

"Mr Dyson, I want you to know how upset I am by Sir Robert's disappearance," she announced. "And I hope I can help you."

We shook hands. "How did you know me?" I asked.

"Robert told me about you," she said. She raised her eyebrows almost flirtatiously. "Glancing around this room, you were the only possibility."

"I don't know why Robert should mention me."

She settled herself in a chair and pushed her glasses up onto her forehead. "He said you were his right hand and if I couldn't get hold of him, I should speak to you."

"You had business with him?"

"Oh, yes. I thought you would know. He is helping with the ordering of medical supplies from Britain to equip field hospitals on the border for 'Doctors without Borders'."

"Just the thing I should have known about and yet I know nothing," I said. I ordered two Americanos from an over-attentive waiter.

She smiled disarmingly. "I can't help that. It is in the early stages."

"I've seen a video of you in a corridor of the Sheraton with Robert, entering the room where Petrie, his security man, was murdered."

"Robert and I had a meeting there. Afterwards, I left and went back to my office."

"Why meet in a bedroom?"

"It was a suite." She spoke soothingly. "We sat at the table. There were easy chairs. It was cooler and cheaper than a meeting room."

She seemed to have all the answers. "Why did a man with a terrorist record, Gafoor Khan, enter that room after you?"

"I don't know. A number of people entered and left. I thought they were staff." She leaned back, completely confident and still with that faintly alluring smile.

I felt frigid. She was a strange and very dangerous woman, but indeed, a beautiful creature. She seemed to be beckoning me on in a seductive way. It would be a leap beyond my capability from here to her arms. I was getting nowhere. A red light flashed in my mind. "I don't believe you, Dr Abdali."

She looked sympathetic. "Mr Dyson, I know how disturbed you must be by Robert's disappearance and Mr Petrie's murder. Things don't add up…"

I swallowed the last of my coffee. "Listen, I've seen the High Commission's Top Secret files. I've seen the reports written by you in your capacity as a spy and an informer. Reports about Robert. You led him into a trap set up by Gerald Macbeth…"

I watched her face carefully as I spoke, but she showed nothing except an amused incomprehension. She replaced her cup, put her hand around the small handbag in her lap and stood up, perfectly calm.

"You are in absolute fantasy land, Mr Dyson. You are overwrought and you need help. Medical help. I must go now." Her words were carefully articulated in a quiet but meaningful voice. She walked away, poised and unruffled.

I dropped a ten dollar note on the table and followed her. I was acting on passionate impulse. If I had stopped to think, I would have realized that our meeting was over. Nothing was to be gained but an ugly scene. I caught up with her on the street and blocked her way. "You're not going to be able to walk away from what you've done!"

"Leave me alone! I had nothing to do with Robert's death!" She spoke vehemently, her cheeks pale. She backed away from me.

"What have you said?"

Her eyes showed a spark of fear. She turned and ran.

35

Robbins came to my office unannounced mid-morning the next day. He was excited; it showed in the jerky movements of his arms and hands. I had rarely seen him display emotion.

"We've pinpointed Sir Robert's location. The intelligence is strong."

"You're sure you don't mean the location where we can collect Robert's body?"

"There's no need to be negative about it. We're still within the IF's time limit."

"I think he's dead."

"Why change your tune suddenly? You're the one who's always saying we have to believe he's alive."

"Dr Abdali told me yesterday that she wasn't responsible for Robert's death."

"Oh, hell! Don't let's get into that again."

"She seemed to know."

"Listen, Nick. I'll go right back to my office and get on with the job if you don't want to be involved."

"All right. Where is he?"

"On one of the tributaries of the Indus. In a floating village. It's a fair way away."

"What's your plan?" At last, Robbins seemed to be on the move.

"I'm going to take a small party out there now. Do you want to be included?" He didn't sound very encouraging.

"How do you feel about that?" I said, not really minding

what he thought. I was so committed to the investigation that I couldn't refuse. However, I wanted a little time to consider while I tried to shut my mind to the danger.

"I don't care one way or the other," Robbins said, woodenly.

"Why are you making the offer?"

"Because you've criticised every move I've made and you'll squeal if I don't give you the opportunity to come."

"Yes, I would squeal. So I'll come."

I made a quick visit to my apartment to pick up slacks, training shoes and a T-shirt, and met Robbins back at his office. We left almost immediately; we were a team of six, including three Pakistani police and Robbins' young Special Branch assistant. We drove for over three hours in two Land Rovers, hammering along rutted tracks and through marshes. It was evening when we arrived at the wide tributary and my body ached from the cramped vehicle and the bruising ride.

The six of us embarked in the moonlight in an old fishing dory with a weary engine.

"Can't you do better than this?" I said to Robbins.

"Arriving in a police powerboat is just what we don't want to do," he said.

Half an hour on the water and we were near to the inlet from the main stream, which was crammed with hundreds of boats. The inlet was brimming from all of the recent rain. These craft, moored against each other, carpeted the water, rising and falling in the swells. Feeble lights lit the boats, many of which were occupied as family homes.

Robbins, using night glasses, identified the hulk that, according to his information, held Robert.

"We only have an hour if the IF timetable means anything," I said. I had resolved to believe Robert was alive.

"They won't be all that precise," Robbins said.

"We shouldn't assume…"

"Take it easy," Robbins said. "Safety first. We'll get him in time."

The minutes ticked by while Robbins waited for a radio call from one of his observers. "Listen, man," I said, after five more minutes had passed, "Robert's going to be dead unless we get our arses in gear!"

Our boat pitched and drifted at the mouth of the inlet. I judged we were at least five, perhaps fifteen, minutes away from the vessel we had to board. We would have to approach it over the decks of other boats.

"I think we should go in," I said, pushing the Pakistani sergeant away from the tiller and opening the throttle. The boat surged forward and the motor stalled.

"You damn fool. You're jeopardising everything!" Robbins said, pulling me away.

The sergeant ground the starter motor heavily in an attempt to fire the engine. The boat drifted in the current from the mouth of the inlet. The starter motor was failing, turning the engine ever more slowly, but at last the engine fired. It came to life with a reluctant growl in a cloud of filthy diesel smoke. The boat nosed up the stream under full throttle and then at half throttle across the inlet. Robbins got his expected message and watched for a suitable landing near the hulk. Our boat smoothed quietly alongside a deserted vessel, which was part of the tight flotilla. Robbins and his boarding party of three jumped on to the net-strewn deck, with machine guns cradled in their arms. They bounded forward across other decks onto the hulk and kicked in the cabin door. I remained on our boat. Robbins and the party returned immediately and he announced that nobody was on board.

There was a sudden cacophony of yelling from another

small craft around a 100 yards away. Lamps were flashing. Small boats were pulling up to it. Excited voices were calling from boat to boat.

"They've found a body in the water," the sergeant said.

I could see two men with boat hooks, silhouettes against the sheen of the water. Robbins headed our dory for the boat. My insides knotted. The men with boat hooks had failed to get the body, whose head and shoulders were now showing in the tide. As we drew near, they raised their hooks from the water in acknowledgment that the tide would have its way.

The body was drifting away from the oily calm where we were and was being drawn toward the rip in the tide. Once in the rip, it would probably submerge and then be drawn into the main stream of the Indus. Robbins watched. A shower of rain prickled the water.

"What are you doing, for Christ's sake? That's almost certainly Robert and he may yet be alive!" I shouted.

"We can't take the boat into the rip. It'll founder and we'll all be drowned."

Robbins directed the sergeant to come alongside the boat that had possibly contained Robert. He prepared to board. The rain pounded hard on my forehead now. I had only a few seconds to make a decision, although my deliberations at the time seemed ponderous and slow. Perhaps Robbins was just being sensible. It would be dangerous to pursue the body and take the boat into the rip, but there was a possibility that the body was Robert's and that he was still alive.

I kicked off my shoes and slipped out of my jeans. I dived overboard. The water was cold and the shock made it clearer for me to measure what I was doing. I swam strongly towards Robert.

I thought my action would force Robbins to bring the boat close to, if not into, the rip tide. All my hours at the Abbey's swimming pool had not been entirely wasted. I was able to follow the bobbing shadow of the body easily and quickly covered the 30 yards to reach it. I grasped the collar as the head loomed before me. Yes, it was Robert, the shape of the skull and the profile were enough for me. It was a strange feeling of triumph, after all we had done together, to be able to grasp him and make him secure.

I was conscious of the boiling sound of the deluge from above hitting the water, pock marking the surface. As soon as I began to struggle back toward the boat, I could feel the frightening pull of the undertow, like a soft hand caressing me and drawing me back. Robbins was steering the boat toward me. A crewman in the bow had a white lifebelt. I swam on my back and side, using one arm to hold Robert and the other to stroke. I thrust forward, kicking strongly. I was beginning to tire. Some of the sensation had gone from my thrashing legs. I was being drawn back and down by that compelling hand.

I had a sudden thought that I should let Robert go. My consciousness was reeling. I felt a rope fall across my head like a blow. I clamped my free hand onto the rope and closed my eyes against the blinding light from the searchlight on the bow of the boat.

I was hauled out of the river half-conscious and vomiting water. Our boat was pitching and rolling uncontrollably in the tide. The craft listed suddenly, taking water over the side. I was flung into the scuppers with Robert. The boat righted when the crew jumped the opposite way. The craft fought its way slowly and tiredly back to the calm water on the other side of the rip.

"We nearly lost it, you asshole!" Robbins shouted,

when we had passed through the line of frothing ripples that marked the tides.

I looked only at what I had saved. It was Robert's muscular body, still wearing the dark blue gaberdine trousers of the suit he had had on when he was taken, a torn and filthy white shirt, bare feet and a golden beard. Despite the movement of the deck, there was a stillness about the body. Robert's mouth oozed slime. A deep red gash flared from his temple. His cheeks were waxen yellow and the open eyes, empty windows.

Robert was indisputably dead. I tried to fit this scene of a beaten and drowned man, a creature from a fisherman's net, with the glorious sun-radiating Robert Laidlaw in life. I put my hand to my temple, thinking I was deluded. The rain drenched us both.

36

I was present at a meeting with Hall and Robbins at the Special Branch offices when Hall confirmed the result of the post-mortem. Robert had died from a severe beating he had received before entering the water, probably well before midnight.

"So Dr Abdali was right. Robert was already dead," I said, though neither of the two cops did more than cast jaundiced glances in my direction.

"Nobody except the next of kin will know anyway," Robbins said.

"Know what?" I asked.

"The exact details of the two deaths," Hall said. "We've said publicly that the body was recovered from the river. There's no point in feeding the details to the press. Emma Laidlaw agrees. Petrie's family in England felt the same about his death."

"So it's all conveniently over," I said, getting up to go. "What about charges against the IF people? Won't it come out there?"

"There won't be any charges," Hall said. "The men arrested on the boat were only stooges providing shelter. The jihadis had all fled."

"What about Macbeth setting up the kidnap and murder?"

The two men scoffed. "There's no evidence of that..." Hall said.

"Yes, there is…"

"No evidence that would stand up in court," Hall said, emphatically, with his yellow smile.

"What about Abdali's role?"

"For shit sake, man, she was just Laidlaw's girlfriend," Hall snarled.

"She set Robert up."

"No evidence," snapped Hall.

"Yes, there is: the video and the Top Secret files."

"I'm sure the government would be very pleased to make our Top Secret files available in a Pakistan criminal court."

The final meeting of the High Commission steering group on the case took place the next day at our regular time. The day was cooler and less humid than usual. The room was laden with red flowers. Sir Hugh Leighton, at ease, swayed before us. He made a brief mention of Robert at the beginning, which gave the impression that when this formality was done we could return to our iced lime juices.

"Naturally, we all regret what has happened. It's very sad. However, I think we had come to reconcile ourselves with losing Robert over recent weeks."

"How has Lady Laidlaw taken it?" Pottinger asked.

"Well, very saddened, but, as you know, they were never very close," he said, looking at me critically.

Emma's association with me had become a well-used item of gossip.

"It's terribly sad," Grace said. "The FO are satisfied, though, that a scandal has been avoided and our diplomatic work can go on unhindered."

"Oh, yes. We'll charge on," Bradshaw said. "Our reputation unblemished."

Hall and Robbins were not smiling, but seemed smoothly relaxed at the ideal solution that had unfolded.

Leighton said, "I want to congratulate you, Leonard, and also Dennis. A damn good effort in difficult circumstances and I'll be commending you both in my report."

"Excellent," Grace echoed.

Pottinger nodded effusively, but Bradshaw and I remained mute.

"I'm afraid I don't agree," I said, when the flurry of congratulations had subsided.

They swivelled to look at me with distaste. Without Robert, I was a much reduced person and they did not have to conceal their contempt quite so carefully. The question whether I was going to make an official complaint remained. Leighton felt strengthened by the recovery of Robert's body. In a sense, he could claim he had found Robert.

"You're a relative newcomer here, Nick, and I don't think you fully understand the difficulties…" he said in a conciliatory tone.

"With a more energetic and better planned investigation, I believe Robert could have been saved."

Leighton turned to the others with a heavy sigh and an edgy smile, trying to convey with an airy wave of his hand that what I had said was unworthy of further comment.

"What about the role of Gerald Macbeth in this? And Celia Abdali? They could be facing charges of counselling and procuring kidnap and murder."

My words did not seem to be heard by anybody present. Leighton sighed again and held up his hand. "Enough," he said.

We filed out to lunch on the veranda. I should have refused to join the others and left the Residence, but the soft tide of relief among the group carried me along. I soon had a large gin and tonic in front of me and sat quietly, appreciating its bluish coldness.

The newspapers already carried the columns I had envisaged. The tragedy, they said, was the botched work of a little-known group of terrorists. The demand for the release of prisoners was not mentioned, which saved explanations about what we had not done with the Pakistan authorities. There was no suggestion that the investigation itself had been botched. The abduction and murder of Sir Robert Laidlaw, the Prime Minister's special envoy, was a fringe outrage– horrifying today, but forgotten tomorrow.

37

I had booked flights for Emma and myself to London. Emma was agreeable in the sense that she didn't say no and knew the flight plans. I thought she was reconciling herself to it and I was sure that it was for her own good, even ahead of my selfish wish to continue an intimate relationship with her.

The FO wound up my employment quickly and I said goodbye to my High Commission colleagues. Rashida was upset at my departure, but stoical. Rather pointedly, but not unexpectedly, neither Leighton or Grace held the usual farewell drinks gathering, but Bradshaw and I had a hearty dinner at the Pakistan Club and too many cognacs afterwards.

I had checked with Emma two days before we were due to fly that she was packing. She remained open to my arrangements, but was sadly lacking in commitment. I kept in touch with her on the telephone and took her to dinner, but only slept with her occasionally at her wish. Not sleeping together worried me, but I said nothing.

On the morning of the flight, I took a cab to her apartment. When the servant admitted me, I walked through to the lounge. Boxes and cases were scattered through the rooms. I found her in the dining room. She was glowing, but she flinched awkwardly when she saw me.

Something was wrong. "I hope you've got somebody to take charge of all this stuff, Emma, because our plane goes in a few hours."

She looked away from me for a moment, without speaking. She then raised her chin and turned to look at me. "Gerry and I are going away, Nick. Isn't it wonderful!"

I had anticipated weeks ago that she might renege on her promise to come to London with me, but this sudden turnaround was unbelievable. I could see the tantalising shape of her breasts through the thin silk dress she was wearing. Her words were obtuse, impossible. If nothing else, though, she was always candid with me. After all the persuading and cajoling and all the arrangements I had made with her, she was telling me now, for the first time, that she was going away with another man. It was as though nothing whatever had been agreed between us.

"I know it's a shock for you, Nick. And I really would like to come with you, and I did intend to, because you're such fun, but I want to go with Gerry now. I think I'm in love with him. And I didn't tell you before because… you can be such a bore about Gerry. And I want us to part as friends."

I felt weak, not angry. It was no use accusing Emma of having misled me. She didn't care any more for promises than she did for wasted airline tickets. "Don't be a fool," I said. "Macbeth doesn't love you. He can't. He hates you!"

"You're jealous!" she laughed.

"I admit it, I am. But even if I wasn't, I'd still beg you to leave here, to leave him."

I tried to persuade her. I took her hand and led her over to the couch, pushing aside the objects that cluttered it.

"Emma, nobody could ever forgive what you have done and then love you and marry you. Whenever Macbeth looks at you, the memory of it will always be there. The memory of all the prizes denied to him as a scholar and an athlete; the memory of the shame; the memory of being arrested and transported in a police van; the memory of the court and the judge and the remand cells and the horrific fear of being condemned to prison when he was innocent. You placed Macbeth's youth in jeopardy and cast a shadow over his whole career."

"I never meant to do it…"

"It doesn't matter. You did it. Those feelings will always stir in Macbeth and the closer you are to him, the more real they will be. The fact that he's rich and distinguished in this small Anglo community makes no difference. He's a human being, which is not saying much about his capacity to act decently."

She listened with a small sign of concern on her compressed lips.

"I haven't told you that on New Year's Eve I was thrown out of Macbeth's house. My arse was kicked and I fell in the dirt."

She laughed. "You silly man. You deserved all you got. Barging into somebody else's house!"

"Emma, the point is that before this happened I had a meeting alone with Macbeth in his library. He said he had hoped never, ever to see any of us again– you, me or Robert. He blamed us for everything. I knew he hadn't forgotten and at that moment, he confirmed it from his own mouth. And after this meeting, the taxi that was conveniently waiting to take me away, dropped me in a back alley in Rawalpindi. When I got out of the cab, two men were waiting with the dog that attacked me. Don't tell me that that was a coincidental event. It was plainly organised."

She looked at the floor for a while, as though I was being tiresome. "I think you're wrong. Gerry's not like that. And the dog. That could have been somebody else, like the bomb in your car and the defacing of this room. You're nice, Nick, but you're a bit paranoid. Gerry wouldn't stoop that low."

"Anybody is like that, Emma. And Macbeth has power here to carry out any evil scheme he wants. Robert won the contest at Poole Abbey and Macbeth lost badly. Macbeth has a deadly determination to win here. Robert could never win here and he's paid the ultimate price.

"What a queer way to see it… and anyway how can you know so conclusively?"

"Because this is the way people behave."

"Footle!"

"The fight has been fought all over again here."

She hooted sceptically. "And you say that Gerry was responsible for Robert's abduction!"

"He was responsible. He set up the meeting at the hotel. The jihadis knew where to find Robert. If you think that it was a love tryst that went wrong, think again. Dr Abdali, Robert's girlfriend, is a spy and an informer and a girlfriend of Macbeth. She led him into the trap."

"If what you say is true about Gerry, then why aren't the police taking action against him? Why hasn't Hugh told me?"

"Because Macbeth is too powerful to touch and Abdali is a useful tool for Special Branch."

"Nick, I think you… need help." She shook her head, hopelessly.

"Macbeth also accused Robert of receiving bribes and denounced him to Special Branch. He wanted to ruin Robert, to get him removed. Leighton has even informed the FO of the allegation."

"Perhaps Robert did take bribes. I wouldn't put it past him. Though I never saw any of the money."

"We three should never have come to Islamabad. It was too much like trying to revisit and relive the past, and it doesn't work."

I was exhausted after my outpouring and Emma was unmoved. She was confident that she was paying a debt she owed, one that she was prepared to pay ten times over because of her affection for Macbeth.

"Emma, what was it that made our lives go wrong all those years ago?" I spoke in a moan of desperation, expecting no answers because there were none.

Emma looked at me fondly. There would always be that much on her side. With a sudden wicked look of amusement, she said, "I thought you guessed."

"What do you mean? I only know what I saw that night. I knew Macbeth was the culprit. When you changed your story and told the police that Macbeth didn't do it, the only person left was Robert."

"I never told the police who the other person was. I told them it happened in the dark and I was knocked about and confused."

"It had to be Robert and he never denied it to me. That's right, isn't it?"

"I don't think I'll satisfy your idle curiosity." Her dimples were showing.

"Hardly idle curiosity. Don't you realise how our lives have been affected by what happened that night?"

"Dear old Nick," she said, putting an arm around my shoulders. "You always were Robert's obedient servant, weren't you? Did you ever go to bed with him?"

"Don't be silly."

"I always thought maybe you did, that there was something special between you. I was always a bit jealous of you and Robert."

"Come on, answer my question, Emma. It's important to understand if we can."

"All right. I'll tell you. Nobody in creation knows this except me and one other person. It'll be a secret between us, OK?" she whispered, brushing her lips against mine, childishly enjoying the moment.

"OK, a secret," I said, not expecting to hear anything beyond the facts that were already wired into my mind.

"It's such a long time ago," she began, pausing and making me think that she was going to remain silent. But she went on:"I could never forget.Things were pretty much out of control in the house that night. Robert came to my room.We did it on the bed.As he was dressed and ready to leave, Gerry came in through the window! Chaotic, isn't it? There was a fight between them. I stepped between them and got a black eye for my pains. I screamed. They were tearing at each other like maniacs. I stopped them and got rid of Robert. Gerry wanted to stay. I hadn't locked the door and Robin Lovelace came in…"

"Lovelace?" I asked, bemused.

For a moment, I couldn't remember who Lovelace was. What astonished me was that Emma wasn't blaming Robert. I had held it against him all these years; it had been the grit in our relationship.

"You remember, the new house tutor– dreadfully pale, straight-nosed, with long, girls' hair and lips smoothed out of marble and such a marvellous name. Robin Lovelace. He'd been eyeing me up since he arrived at March House. He was on duty, in charge of the house. Gerry fled out of the window. Robin saw me with hardly any clothes on. He wrapped me in a blanket and carried me to his room. I suppose that was classified as protective. Then, he did it to me in his room. He was awfully rough and he hurt me.

That might have been it, the end, but what we didn't know was that somebody had called the hall and got Larsen to come back. He caught me in Robin's room with a blanket around me and hardly any clothes on underneath. Then, the Head and Uncle Tom Cobley and all arrived. It was a case of please explain."

"And you named Macbeth."

"No. Robin saw that the boy who fled through the window was Macbeth and he named him, pretending he had arrived too late to save a damsel in distress. I thought it might all go away then, but it only got worse. Obviously Robin was expecting me to support him and I had to say something. The Headmaster, Larsen and Matron more or less told me what had happened. When they knew what the doctor found… you know, the abrasions I had… and the doctor recommended calling the police…"

Emma looked now as she probably looked then, the helpless victim of conflicting forces.

"Wasn't there forensic evidence?"

"I didn't get to the police doctor until the following day and I think Robin wore a condom."

"Why didn't you tell the truth, say it was Lovelace and that it wasn't rape, just violent sex?"

"I don't know. He was a master. And if I did tell, he'd be kicked out. I'd have to explain about Gerry and Robert and that I'd been seeing them both. I'd have been kicked out for sure and my family… you know, all that. I wasn't thinking straight. The Head and his team hounded me. All they thought of was the school. I had no idea it would lead to police charges. I thought it would… blow over. After all, I was the one who was supposed to be hurt and I didn't want to make a big fuss."

"Macbeth must hate you."

"He doesn't know anything about Robin. He thinks it was Robert. It's all so mixed up and so long ago."

"Time burnishes hate, Emma."

"You're wrong, Nick, but I'm glad I've told you. I know you care for me. You're like a brother."

A brother, an amusing partner, an exciting lover. I had to accept that this is all I would ever be. I would never connect with her except in the most trifling way. I left her feeling bloated with sadness and frustration. She was fluttering excitedly among her possessions like a bright, exotic bird.

I was astonished, almost shocked, that Robert whom I had always held guilty, was actually innocent.

38

I looked at my watch as the cab wound down from the Langar. I had an hour to make it to the airport. I had given up trying to persuade Emma. I had already pushed my efforts past persuasion to entreaty. She was entirely fixed on what she thought was going to be her new life with Macbeth. I was worried for her safety and grief-stricken, knowing that I might never see her again.

I had a sense of impending disaster for her and for myself, a sense that if I didn't get out of Islamabad soon, a black event would overtake me and I would never be able to leave. Even as the driver threaded in and out of the traffic, I had the hope that I wasn't too late. I longed to hear the scream of the jet engines and be flattened against my seat as the plane accelerated down the runway. Until that moment, my nerves would ache with apprehension.

I paid the driver hurriedly at the airport and gave him all my remaining Pakistani currency. I had shipped most of my few possessions home weeks ago. I carried my one remaining suitcase and a small handbag through the sliding doors toward the check-in desk. I searched the monitors inside for the flight and began to move through the crowd in the right direction. Only then did I realise that three or four men were watching me, ringed out around me, perhaps 10 or 15 feet away, waiting.

One of the watchers was the Rawalpindi casino man, but the others were uniformed Pakistani police and then from behind came the familiar groomed figure of Robbins. He wasn't grinning but there was a peculiar look of excitement and triumph on his face. His thin lips were pressed together and the usually impassive eyes glinted.

"Drop your bags, Nick, you're under arrest."

"Shit!" I said, letting my suitcase fall.

The other cops scurried in to snatch both my bags.

"What's this about?" I asked, excitedly, like an innocent man, but hearing the clang of the trap springing shut in my head.

"You come along with me and we'll talk about it," Robbins replied, clamping my elbow and steering me across the hall to a customs post.

The room was grey-coloured with dull lights and benches, on which the cops dumped my luggage. They began a search, throwing clothes and other possessions on the table and the floor. They worked as though these bags would never have to be repacked.

"You better tell me what the charge is," I said, knowing the police would not behave so arrogantly unless they were sure of their ground. Somewhere, I had made a bad mistake. Something was coming that I hadn't anticipated.

"There's no charge, yet. You're being detained for questioning by the Pakistani police. You're suspected of being an accessory to bribery and receiving the proceeds of bribery. It's very simple. I know you removed bribe money from Robert Laidlaw's safe. You hid it and you're trying to get away with it. I'm going to get one of the officers to search you."

"It can't have been a big sum if you think you can find it in my pocket," I said, trying to be as jaunty as possible.

He motioned the casino man to search me. When my wallet was produced, Robbins went through it carefully. The wallet was thick with travellers' checks and airline tickets, but no deposit receipt for money and no wire transfer document.

"So this is the final move to destroy my credibility and shut me up, is it? You don't want me to get back to Westminster, do you? You're worried that I'm going to expose your incompetence."

"You're raving, Nick. You're being detained on legitimate criminal enquiries."

I was searched very thoroughly; it included the linings of my empty pockets and my underwear. The lining of my suitcase was slit and scrutinised. In my hand baggage all they found was a novel to read on the plane, a woollen sweater, a new Canon digital camera and a last-minute present of embroidered linen I had bought for my aunt. After a few minutes, the furious activity subsided and the men fell back from their task. The corpse of my luggage was lying butchered on the table. What they were looking for, whatever it was, wasn't there.

I took advantage of the moment. "You don't have anything on me, Robbins. You have to find some of this mythical bribe money. You have to trace it to me. You can't, because I never had it."

Robbins considered for a moment and then walked off to an adjoining room. I could hear him making a call. When he came back a few moments later, he said, "All right. You can go. But I bloody well know that you got away with that money. If I ever see you here again, I'll go through your affairs with a microscope."

I ignored him, but I was bursting with relief. I began to stuff my clothes back into the wounded suitcase. I had less than half an hour to get the plane. "If I wasn't leaving the country, I'd make a personal complaint about you and the way you've handled this," I said, sourly. "I may still do so when I get to London."

The plane took off twenty minutes later and when it was cruising at 30,000 feet, I felt my tension melt as the neat whisky began to go to my head. Most of all though, I felt the ache of losing Emma.

39

After that event, there were many nights when I awoke from a nightmare of arrest, a nightmare of a trial as an accessory to bribery, and a nightmare of being sentenced for receiving the proceeds of crime. On some nights I was in the Habib prison, sweating out an interminable sentence. And always, after these bad dreams, there was a rush of warmth, the appreciation that I was free and that it was better to be a modestly successful barrister in London than a potential victim of Macbeth in Islamabad. I wound down my sights on a career; the criminal bar wasn't so bad after all.

I decided not to carry out my threat to lobby for a government enquiry into the Laidlaw abduction; it wouldn't bring Robert back or bring Emma back to me. It probably wouldn't show that Macbeth was instrumental in Robert's abduction and murder. I hadn't the necessary malice in me against Grace Stewart and Leighton to sustain the energy I would need for the task.

And there was always the comfort of spending the money! The new Mercedes 300SK sports, my elegant Chelsea apartment, even the Dom Perignon was so much more exquisite when I viewed it as a present from Gerald Macbeth and a recompense for being kicked out of his house and bitten by his dog.

My unwitting part in Macbeth's disgrace didn't trouble me, but I shivered at the thought of our lives being swerved this way and that by small, seemingly inconsequential events, or distorted by mistakes and misunderstandings. In setting events in train, Macbeth was certainly more innocent, one could say, than Robert or Lovelace. Circumstance and coincidence had caught Macbeth in a trap, and after torturing him for months, had poisoned his youth forever. And Lovelace, that unknown and only half-remembered tutor, whose lust and lies had engineered the tragedy; well, his intervention had been more animal than human. It was a baleful force at the edge of our lives. However, Robert, Emma, Lovelace and I had obliviously created a monster in Macbeth.

My high life in London was spoiled by Emma's absence. There were other women, of course. I met and loved more than one woman of quality, who was physically alluring, educated, sensible, caring and seemingly an ideal mate, but Emma never left my thoughts. I had no illusions about her faults. She was trivial and selfish and a deceiver, but she remained for me a rough-cut jewel, a ruby, of little use from a practical point of view, yet a magnetic object of desire.

I wrote begging her to change her mind and return to London. My letters were couched in delicate terms, but I was imploring her.

She replied during the first few months, with postcards full of breathless comments. 'Having a marvellous time!' or 'Just back from Verbier!' And later there were cards, which showed, I thought, a change in tone. 'I think of our good times together' or 'How's dirty old London?' The last card mentioned that she was planning a holiday in London. Then, the cards stopped. I wrote to her every few weeks but received no answers.

After an empty space of about six months, I decided to get in touch with her parents in Salisbury. I spoke to her father on the telephone, explaining that I was an old friend whose letters weren't being answered. My nerves were drawn tight. I was ready for the worst. To me, the worst would be that she had settled down with a man (it surely could never be Macbeth) and had had a baby, although in another part of my heart I wished happiness for her without me.

When I made my enquiry, I knew at once from her father's quavery hesitation that something had happened that he found difficult to talk about. He wasn't being uncooperative. He seemed unsure that he could talk about it to a stranger on the telephone. Clearly, it wasn't marriage. It couldn't be a happy event. I waited anxiously on the line, my guts griping, while Mr Southern gathered his resolve.

He eventually said, "I'm afraid Emma died in an accident a few months ago. She's buried here, in Salisbury."

Although this kind of news was something I had contemplated in the darkest hour of night, my breath choked at the reality. The old man was too upset to talk. I ended the conversation by explaining that I had known Emma in Islamabad and asked permission to visit the family and pay my respects.

I felt a gaping chasm of loss, as personal as if Emma had been living with me. Hardly a day had gone by since Islamabad when I hadn't thought of her. Then, I became angered and morbidly curious to learn what had happened, because of the chill of Macbeth's enmity.

A fortnight after the phone conversation, the Southerns left a message at my chambers inviting me to afternoon tea at the weekend. Understandably, they didn't want to talk about the death during my visit. All they said was that it had been a swimming accident. They simply accepted it. They were pleased when I talked about Emma and some of the times we spent together. After, I went to the graveyard with flowers. Young grass was already sprouting from Emma's plot. The modest headstone recorded nothing beyond dates and that she was the beloved daughter of her parents.

I found it hard to believe that she could be at my feet. Emma, with all her thrilling life force, was literally under the soil a few feet down– or rather what was left of her. I couldn't reconcile this barren moment with the flame that had tortured me.

Almost coldly, dispassionately, as I drove back to London, I realised that I couldn't leave the story as it rested now. I had to know more. Back in my chambers at the Inner Temple, I made enquiries and was given the name of reliable private enquiry agents in Islamabad. I telephoned and wrote to them, requesting a full report on the circumstances leading to the death of Lady Emma Laidlaw. After six weeks, I received a thick dossier. The enquiry agents justified their huge fee with bulk. It arrived in the late afternoon post. I reluctantly put it aside until my colleagues left in the evening. I read the report at my desk with complete absorption when the chambers were silent.

The report actually revealed very little, although reading between the lines was painful. Enquiries from perhaps ten people gave a picture of Emma in the months before her death.

She was described in the report as an attractive and popular woman who had occupied a luxury apartment in Chundra Road. She had been a frequent guest at embassy parties and the homes of the wealthy. A few months before she died, it was suggested that she was in financial difficulty – strange, in view of her pension and compensation from the British Government. She had moved to a smaller apartment in Husseinabad and from there to a shared apartment with two women employed by British Airways. In the newspaper reports enclosed, there were hints of drug abuse that really went no further than saying that she had attended parties where drugs were used. She had worked for a while as a clerk at Pakistani Airlines. This employment had ended. The word 'dismissed' wasn't used.

Emma was killed at a Sunday boat party at Manora Island, Karachi on the weekend before she was due to leave for London. She was a strong swimmer who had ventured far from the boat, into the path of a water-ski speedboat. The driver did not see her and the boat passed over her, causing fatal injuries with its hull and propellers. Copies of newspaper reports headed 'Swimming Party Tragedy' and 'Socialite Killed by Speedboat' were attached and brought back to me the disquiet I had had when I was with Emma at a similar party.

A copy of the coroner's finding, death by accident, was also attached with a note of the hearing. The driver of the speedboat was an experienced boat-hand and water-ski driver. No direct blame was attached to him, although the coroner observed that such powerful boats ought not to be operated in areas used for swimming. A copy of the death certificate described Emma's injuries. The blades of the propellers had lacerated her skull fatally, splitting it open.

The host at the boat party was named in the newspaper reports as Gerald Macbeth.

At the end, the papers dropped from my fingers to the floor. I felt the oppression of the bookshelves around me and an inexpressible hollowness. When I came to myself, the windows were dark and I was cold to the bone.